P

What an ~~adventure. A mix of dragons, shipwrecks and~~ *science,*
perfect for 8+. It has that classic tale feel, like Treasure Island,
and is gripping from first to last. Plus, lizard puppy!

LOUIE STOWELL

. . . an epic Victorian adventure in which science and fantasy collide.
Brilliantly written, and it has real heart too.

LUCY STRANGE

A striking and original adventure weaving magic with
science, history and hugely likeable characters.

EMMA CARROLL

I loved Darwin's Dragons *. . . It's a stunner.*

FLEUR HITCHCOCK

. . . the beautifully fictionalised story of Syms Covington,
a cabin boy during Darwin's voyage on the HMS Beagle.

THE TELEGRAPH

PRAISE FOR *MY FRIEND THE OCTOPUS*

Colourful historical detail sets the scene for an intriguing crime thriller . . .

THE DAILY MAIL

Set in 1893, this is historical fiction with oodles of charm and adventure.

IRISH INDEPENDENT

A wonderfully atmospheric story . . . A powerful tale
of friendship and self-discovery.

THE i

A MESSAGE FROM CHICKEN HOUSE

Lindsay Galvin writes fantastic stories about what *might* have happened around some pretty well-known events. So, what connects a dog, a stowaway, a sea serpent and a survivor with that most famous tragedy at sea? Well, not what you might expect! But these ingredients make for the most brilliant story – where lots of real facts rub shoulders with a wonderful tale of animal friendship and mysterious sightings!

BARRY CUNNINGHAM
Publisher
Chicken House

Call of the
TITANIC

LINDSAY GALVIN

Chicken House

2 PALMER STREET, FROME,
SOMERSET BA11 1DS
WWW.CHICKENHOUSEBOOKS.COM

Text © Lindsay Galvin 2023
Cover and interior illustration © Gordy Wright 2023

First published in Great Britain in 2023
Chicken House
2 Palmer Street
Frome, Somerset BA11 1DS
United Kingdom
www.chickenhousebooks.com

Chicken House/Scholastic Ireland, 89E Lagan Road, Dublin Industrial Estate,
Glasnevin, Dublin D11 HP5F, Republic of Ireland

Cover and interior design by Steve Wells
Typeset by Dorchester Typesetting Group Ltd
Printed and bound in Great Britain by CPI Group (UK) Ltd, Croydon CR0 4YY

1 3 5 7 9 10 8 6 4 2

British Library Cataloguing in Publication data available.

PB ISBN 978-1-913696-69-6
eISBN 978-1-915026-59-0

*To all those who put themselves
in danger to help others.*

Also by Lindsay Galvin

Darwin's Dragons
My Friend the Octopus
The Secret Deep

RMS *Titanic* set sail on her maiden voyage
on 10th April 1912.

She sank at 2.20 a.m. on 15th April 1912
in the North Atlantic.

There were not enough lifeboats for
all the passengers and crew. One thousand
four hundred and ninety-six died.

Over seven hundred survived,
escaping in eighteen lifeboats.

The *Titanic* survivors were rescued
by RMS *Carpathia*.

Many survivors of the disaster were required
to give evidence at inquiries in New York,
Washington DC and London, to find out why
so many people died. Young steward Sidney
Daniels escaped *Titanic* but was never called
for evidence. I have written his fictionalized
story guided by the style of the many witness
statements I read for research.

27th

April

1912

(Twelve days after RMS *Titanic* was lost)

UNITED STATES SENATE INQUIRY

Day 9 - 27th April 1912
Testimony of Sidney Daniels
(The Witness was Duly Sworn by Senator
Bourne)

SENATOR BOURNE: Please be seated, Mr Daniels.
My name is SENATOR BOURNE and this is my
stenographer, Mrs Perry, who will be taking a
record of your testimony in shorthand. She
will then type up the testimony for you to sign
so it can be added to the official record.

- Yes, sir, I understand.

SENATOR BOURNE: All I ask is that you answer
my questions in full and truthfully. Leave no
detail out.

- Yes, sir.

SENATOR BOURNE: Then I think we are ready to
begin. For the record. Is your name Sidney
Daniels?

- Yes, sir.

SENATOR BOURNE: Were you a third-class steward on the Titanic?

- Yes, sir.

SENATOR BOURNE: How old were you when serving on the Titanic, son?

- Fifteen, sir.

SENATOR BOURNE: What were you doing at the time of the collision?

- I was off duty and in my bunk, sir.

SENATOR BOURNE: On which deck was your cabin?

- E deck, sir. Off the main working corridor we called Scotland Road.

SENATOR BOURNE: Is it a cabin in which a number of third-class stewards are berthed together? A dormitory-type arrangement?

- Yes, sir.

SENATOR BOURNE: What is it you are holding in your hand, Mr Daniels?

- It's just some letters I wrote my ma, sir. I never got a chance to post them and I thought if you ask me about the days running up to the disaster . . . well, I might not remember with all that's happened, but it's in here.

SENATOR BOURNE: I think it might be helpful for an impression of how third class was operating before the incident.

Mrs Perry, please clearly mark when Mr Daniels is reading from his private correspondence.

- You want me to read out loud? Sorry, sir, it's just . . . well, it's a letter to my ma. And you know, she worries. So it might not be any use, it's not all official like . . .

SENATOR BOURNE: I understand, but I would like to hear all the same. What mattered to you matters to this inquiry. Would you prefer Mrs Perry to read?

- Goodness no, sir! She probably couldn't make sense of my handwriting, sir, Ma always does say I have a bit of a scrawl.

SENATOR BOURNE: Very well. And remember, Mr Daniels, we are not judging you or anyone else at this stage before the accident; this was just one more ship, full of people with mothers, just like yours.

Wednesday

10th

April

1912

Dear Ma,

Can you believe I am writing from RMS Titanic! Quite the crowd at Southampton dock, but I was sure I could see you waving.

We've already loaded the passengers at Cherbourg and now off to Queenstown in Ireland.

All the stewards have now been given a section to look after. Mine is the single men's where the biggest challenge is barely anyone speaks English. Most are seeking a new life in America and starting in style on a ship like this! Each third-class cabin has four bunks with comfortable bedding, many have their own portholes, there is even running water in each cabin. They can't believe their eyes.

The other stewards seem a rum lot, but won't be too much time for larks with us scrubbing and mopping cabins dawn 'til dusk. I am not the youngest here, there's a bellboy who is just fourteen, so you needn't fret. I've not had a chance to explore the decks – but I will find a way although hope I don't get lost. It is like being on a floating city.

I'm folding in a copy of the third-class menu

for you to see – isn't it quite the feast? The roast beef for dinner was the finest most passengers have ever had! And it isn't so different for the stewards, just a bit less choice. Best thing is, chef knows how to do a good rice pud, but not as good as yours, Ma.

Now the other chaps are readying for their beds so I must turn off the light.

Your loving son,
Sid

WHITE STAR LINE.

R.M.S. "TITANIC."   APRIL 14, 1912.

THIRD CLASS.

BREAKFAST.

OATMEAL PORRIDGE & MILK
SMOKED HERRINGS, JACKET POTATOES
HAM & EGGS
FRESH BREAD & BUTTER
MARMALADE   SWEDISH BREAD
TEA   COFFEE

DINNER.

RICE SOUP

FRESH BREAD   CABIN BISCUITS
ROAST BEEF, BROWN GRAVY
SWEET CORN   BOILED POTATOES
PLUM PUDDING, SWEET SAUCE
FRUIT

TEA.

COLD MEAT
CHEESE   PICKLES
FRESH BREAD & BUTTER
STEWED FIGS & RICE
TEA

SUPPER.

GRUEL   CABIN BISCUITS   CHEESE

Any complaint respecting the Food supplied, want of attention or incivility, should be at once reported to the Purser or Chief Steward. For purposes of identification, each Steward wears a numbered badge on the arm.

CLARA

Montgomery, New York State, Scott Ranch

I murmur to Folly, stroking her cheek as I settle her saddle. A ripple of irritation passes across her chestnut flanks but there's barely a snicker from her. When a beam of light passing through the barn roof hits her glossy mane, I smile. I was right to choose her; Papa warned she'd be a hot one, but she's getting better all the time.

'You just need someone willing to take a few risks, don't you, girl?' I say.

I move my face into the light and close my eyes for a moment. This is the day I've been jazzed about for so long. A quick trail ride along the hillside tracks with Folly, then off with Papa on the cart to fetch my English cousin Harold Cottam from the station. Harry is only in New York for a few days and can fit one quick overnight visit to our ranch before his next transatlantic voyage. He is the telegraph operator on the steamship RMS *Carpathia*.

His last telegram is in my skirt pocket. When I rummage for it, Folly raises her top lip and snuffles, hoping for a peppermint candy.

'Not for you, girl,' I say, reading the words.

Arriving at Montgomery 3 p.m. 10th April with much excitement. Harold Cottam.

The curl-edged paper is ridged by my pencil pressing on the back, where I transferred the message into the dots and dashes of Morse code that Harry would have sent from his Marconi telegraph machine aboard *Carpathia*. It amazes me how words can now fly across oceans just by sounding the long and short beeps on the Marconi machine and the operator at the other end converting them back to words.

I smile at Cousin Harry using his full name as if our family wouldn't know who he was. Papa always reads out his letters after dinner and then I'm allowed to have them to read over and over again. When I was smaller I admit that I used to play at being Harry, wearing my brother's knickerbockers, pretending the horses were the exotic animals he saw on his travels. I blush a bit to think of that; of course I've grown out of it now.

Harry is the only person I know who has travelled further than New York. Since I last saw him, he's been to Australia. Australia! I need to know *everything*. All the things he's seen and done. I hope he doesn't find us at Scott Ranch downright boring. Wouldn't blame him if he did.

'Clara! Swell, you're here,' calls my oldest brother Frank, strutting into the stables like the big shot just because he's helping Papa manage the farm now. 'Father needs you to go to Three Pine Ridge and fetch back 203, she's too near her time. She should have been penned earlier.'

I stare at him, hand on hip. Escorting a trundling pregnant cow is not part of my plan today. Being the baby of the family can be a drag, but at least I've been mostly left to do as I please, being considered too young for most chores. I don't much like the way that situation is changing as I get older.

'Darn it, Frankie,' I whine, 'can't one of the others do it?'

''Fraid not, sis, all hands at the pump,' he says, already turning, clicking his fingers to our herding dog, Peg. 'Go with Clara.'

Peg runs over and sits obediently at my feet, ears cocked.

'What's eating you? Peg's got half a brain, she knows what to do,' says Frank, with a grin.

I glare at him. 'I know what to do!' I snap, indignant. 'But I'm going with Papa to fetch Harry,' I say, annoyed to hear the catch in my voice.

Frank checks his watch and shrugs. 'Get a wiggle on and you'll be back by the time he arrives. And a pregnant heifer will be safe.'

I open my mouth to argue, then catch Folly's gleaming eye. An idea. If I take Folly she'll be fast enough. The young horse isn't used to Peg, or to herding the cows, but she can learn on the job—

'Papa said you're to go on Bess,' says Frank, thumbs in his braces.

I can't help myself and know I'm far too old for it by far, but I stamp my foot. 'Bess is as slow as a slug,' I wail. 'I'll never be back in time . . .'

Frank blows into the stout old mare's grey whiskered nose. 'And solid with it. Poor Bess, Clarty Clara doesn't mean it. Slow and steady wins the race, doesn't it, lady? Maybe you can teach little sis a thing or two.'

I glare at the dust motes spinning as Frank sweeps out, and stamp my foot again. So now they've decided I'm old enough for this chore or that, yet when it suits them they treat me like a baby who can't even decide which horse is best.

I'll fetch that cow to the stable, exercise my mare *and* make it back in time to meet Harry.

I check Frank has really gone, then lead Folly out of her stall, lowering my shoulders and forcing my voice to a calm whisper; Folly can always tell when I am upset and I don't want her distracted. Peg cocks her head to one side and I ruffle between her ears.

'This is a load of horsefeathers, Peg. But we'll show them.'

2

ack at the ranch with the heifer finally in the barn, I dash through the back stable door and whip off Folly's saddle. Her sides tremble and I pat her, my mind racing. I'm so late! Harry will likely already be up at the farmhouse. There'll be no chance to talk with him on his own, to ask the questions about his adventures I've been storing up for so long.

But I can't leave Folly like this.

Sweat beads on my forehead as I race to hang and polish my horse's tack and grab the curry brush for the quickest of grooms. She's content with her oats and I'm pleased enough with my work.

I might get away with no one ever knowing I took Folly instead of Bess.

All in all Folly did well for her first time with our cattle dog Peg by her side. On the way up to Three Pine Ridge I thought I might even make it back in time to go with Papa to fetch Harry. But when Peg started herding the pregnant heifer, darting and yipping, Folly startled. Once the wind was up her she tugged at the reins, and galloped. When she finally stopped we were on the edge of the farmstead boundary.

I had to lead Folly on foot all the way back, Peg and the heifer way out in front, every step more impatient than the last.

Still, the job is done.

Now I get to see Harry!

With one last blow into Folly's velvety nostrils, I whisper, 'Not your fault, girl, you'll do better next time,' then lift my skirts and race out of the stable, flinging the door closed behind me, my grin spreading wide as I skip across the courtyard to the farmhouse, finally free.

I swing open the front door, following voices to the parlour, making out Harry's English accent. I push the parlour door open harder than I mean to, so it slams into the wall. My whole family are there, but I see nothing but Harry, in his ship's uniform, cap tilted over his brow.

It's like all my dreams of adventure are here, parcelled up in one person. He stands and I rush over to him, only just preventing myself from running into his arms – after all, I am twelve now – but taking his hand in both of mine and shaking it hard.

'Little Cousin Clara! Can that really be you?' says Harry, as I finally release him.

'Well, one might be forgiven for asking,' says Ma in a dangerous voice. I try to ignore it.

'Did you see kangaroos? In Australia? Did you see koala bears and crocodiles?' I blurt out.

Harry smiles with a little shake of his head, his grey eyes laughing.

Ma stands, shimmering in her green dress, and glides in front of him before he can answer. It's only now I notice Ma's and my sisters' fresh frocks with no aprons, Father in his suit, and even my brothers with scrubbed faces and clean white collars. It hadn't dawned on me we'd be in Sunday best.

'Clara!' says Ma sharply. 'Wait for me in the hall, please.'

I blink. 'But Ma, Harry—'

She ushers me out of the door. Her dark green eyes are stony and her Irish accent grows stronger. 'The state of you, Clara. The very state of you, my mother would turn in her grave to see I've raised such a wild and wilful hinny. No thought for the rest of us, no thought at all.'

'I'm sorry, Ma, but Harry is hardly likely to care about my clothes . . .'

The parlour door opens and Papa closes it behind him, shutting out the cheerful voices inside.

Double horsefeathers. It's a rare and sorry day I'm ticked off by *both* parents at once. I stare at the polished floor where a ring of dust has settled around me as the mud dries, wanting to get this over as quickly as possible. Pa can't know I took Folly, so how bad can a telling-off about a dress really be?

'Look at me, Clara, please,' says Pa. He's using his quiet voice, but I am not fooled. I swallow and do as he says, making my face as repentant as possible. His greying hair is neatly divided in a sharp line, his blue eyes soft above ruddy cheeks.

'Sorry, Papa,' I say.

There is a long moment. A burst of laughter from the parlour. I try not to fidget but it's like an invisible string is pulling me back to my English cousin. To finally have something different to talk about than pregnant heifers, butter churning, milk yields and what needs to be mended. And the weather. I only want to hear about the weather again if it's an avalanche . . . or the boiling desert and how to survive, I bet that's what Harry is talking about right now. I shift from foot to foot in impatience.

'I know you've been looking forward to seeing Harold, Clara, so we are not going to interfere with that.'

I smile. 'Thank you, Papa,' I say. So, not a serious telling-off after all. I turn to head up the stairs.

'But you have scared your mother half to death and with good reason. There must be consequences,' he says.

I sigh and my shoulders slump before I can stop them. Papa draws a deep breath in through his nostrils.

'Did Frank tell you to take Bess?'

I pinch my lips together.

'Now I think about it, he might have said that,' I say carefully. Is it really a lie if it could be true and no one can tell? I could easily have misheard my brother.

'But you took Folly anyway.'

'How did you know?' I burst out, cursing my sneak of an older brother. He must have come back to check I was doing as I was told . . . but when Papa's frown deepens, the words start to babble out of me. 'Folly needed exercise and I knew Bess was tired . . . it was a – sensible decision.'

Father folds his arms. I trail off.

'And this sensible decision, to take an untrained horse out in the fields with the herd – it worked out well, did it?' he says, looking me up and down.

'Quite well!' The last word comes out as a whine, as another peal of laughter comes from the living room.

Mama draws in a sharp breath and I see now the pinched look on her face was worry. 'I told you I wanted to use Folly to turn the butter churn.'

Now I curse myself. Mama had told me earlier. I'd been so excited about Harry coming I'd forgotten. That was how they knew what I'd done.

'My girl. I have been afeared half to distraction and now you can't even grace your own good parents with the truth, let alone look the least bit sorry. I want you clean and *appropriately* dressed before I catch another glimpse of you. And for pity's sake try to do something with that hair.'

Mama turns back into the parlour. I'm left with Pa.

'Clara. I do not complain about your near-always state of disarray, I indulge your interests and allow you much more freedom than your brothers and sisters ever had at your age. But this utter lack of regard for the consequence of your actions . . . and the lies . . .'

'I didn't . . .'

Father ducks to keep my eyes on his. 'If you don't have a care for your own safety, at least consider the animals in your charge.'

I cut off a memory of when Peg snapped at the heifer's shins and Folly started to rear. But I'd managed to calm them, so why be upset about what didn't even happen?

'You will remain inside the house for a week. You will

complete house duties alongside your mother and will only go outside accompanied by one of your brothers or sisters.'

I grind my teeth at the thought but tilt my head to one side. It's a punishment that will send me half wild but it could be worse, as long as I can exercise Folly . . .

'Yes, Papa. After I exercise Folly in the morning, I will do anything Mama asks.' I swing past him, hands on the carved banister. 'Sorry, Pa, I am, thank you. Sorry, really I am, now can I . . .'

'No Folly. I will see to it she is exercised.'

'You can't do that!' I burst out. I know I am being too bold, I know I must stop, but my mouth is a runaway train. 'Folly needs me! I'll get up at dawn to take her out, I'll—'

'You will not see Folly. For a week. If it sets back her training, you only have your own actions to blame.'

I thump up the stairs. This house is a prison. If only I could sail away from it all, like Harry.

3

In my room I swallow back the lump in my throat. Papa can't mean it about me not seeing Folly, he's just mad because I worried Ma. I'll persuade him when he's not so steamed up.

I force myself to look into the mirror and despite my dismay I can't help but laugh.

'Gee, I look like a—'

I really can't think of a word to describe my reflection. My wavy reddish chestnut hair – which I'm rather proud of as it looks like Folly's mane – has blown loose, and now frames my smudged face in a mass of tangles. My white petticoats are brown with dirt, and my forearms streaked with sweat, dust and Folly's foam. I've also trampled in a cowpat, as it crusts one riding boot right up my laces.

I brandish my hairbrush at my reflection. 'This is going to hurt.'

When my scalp aches and my face and neck are glowing from scrubbing, I strip off the stained clothes and truss myself up in my Sunday best, a pale-green checked calico dress that I kind of hate.

Finally I join the others in the parlour. I smile gratefully at my sister Sarah when she shifts so I can sit next to her on the piano stool close to Harry. He grins at me but doesn't stop what he is already talking about and I struggle not to interrupt.

'. . . Well, I bunk down in the wireless room right next to the Marconi telegraph machine. Unlike the bigger ships, there is only one wireless operator on RMS *Carpathia*, and that's me.'

'So you are in sole charge of communications for the whole ship?' says Pa.

Harry nods proudly. He is younger than Frank, barely older than my next brother Gerald.

'Oh, Harold, what with you being the youngest officer to qualify and now in charge – sure my sister must be beside herself with pride,' adds Ma.

'It's a very exciting job, Aunt, and I am glad to do it,' says Harold.

Then Papa asks him about how the Marconi wireless telegraph machine works and images of kangaroos, koalas and crocodiles spin in my head, circling Folly, who I can't see for a whole week.

Finally there's a gap in the conversation.

'Cousin Harry, can you tell us about the animals in Australia?' I say.

My sister Sarah nudges me. 'Oh, Clarty, Harry already told us all about Australia . . .'

I glare at her using my baby name in front of Harry. But Harry's smile is kind.

'That's all right, Sarah. Just outside Sydney we saw two male kangaroos, and honestly they are ten feet tall on their hind legs and they boxed just like . . .'

The bell rings for supper and everyone stands. Sarah links her arm through Harry's on one side, and Ma is on the other.

Dinner feels like a punishment as I'm sat so far from Harry. I'm sent to bed at the usual time, me and my sister before everyone else. In the past I would have got my own way and persuaded Ma and Papa to let us stay up late . . . but today I don't dare argue.

Now I toss and turn.

When Ma sits on the end of my bed I ignore her.

Harry will leave tomorrow, nothing has gone as I imagined, and what will I have to look forward to then? I'm also worried that Papa really means it about Folly; I can't bear to think about not seeing my horse for a whole week. It isn't fair to get punished for something that never actually happened.

'In the morning, you can help me pack the chest with Harry, he's taking Grandmama's things back to your aunt in England. You'll get a chance to talk to Harry on your own then,' says Ma, patting my leg over the covers.

I don't reply, although at least it is something.

'Goodnight, God bless,' says Ma and kisses me on the forehead. I lie rigid. My parents have spoilt everything, and I can't bring myself to reply to her although she always told us never to go to sleep on an argument.

Ma sighs and I hear her kiss my sister, her reply and then the door closes.

'It's not fair to ignore Ma,' says Sarah. 'It's not her fault you deliberately took the wrong horse.'

I roll over, dragging the covers tight around me. 'What's it got to do with you?' I say, cheeks immediately burning. 'You know nothing about horses. All you care about is your stupid cheese and stupid cream.'

In the shocked silence I regret my harsh words, but somehow can't take them back.

The silence stretches tight as horsehair. I bet Sarah cries. She always cries.

Not this time.

'You don't know much about horses yourself, or you wouldn't have taken Folly,' says Sarah.

'Shut your goody two shoes mouth,' I snap.

'You know you spoilt the night for all of us,' says Sarah softly. 'Clarty Clara's antics aren't funny anymore.'

My stomach twists at the thought that Harry might think badly of me, then I let my anger take over, a much better feeling than embarrassment. How dare she? *She* was talking and laughing at the table next to Harry, *she* isn't going to have her first horse ruined all for something that didn't even happen.

'You could never understand – because you're so boring you make me sick!' I hiss.

This time nothing breaks the silence and it seems a long time before I hear Sarah's soft snores.

Finally I give up trying to sleep, my head whirling, so I tiptoe downstairs. I saw off a slice of bread and slick it with butter. I pour some fresh milk from a bottle in the larder. The perks of living on a dairy farm, until you are asked to help with the milking or churning. I'll bet Ma gets me doing that tomorrow. She'll even choose a different horse to turn the wheel for the churn so I don't see Folly.

At the thought of it, anger bubbles up inside me again. I grab a jar of last year's maple syrup – we make our own up from the maple trees that grow behind the ridge – and drizzle it defiantly all over my bread, much more than I'm allowed to have. By the time I've eaten it and tiptoed back to bed, I'm even more wide awake. I don't fall asleep until the blue tinge of dawn is seeping around the edge of the curtains.

I wake to find Sarah's bed neatly made and sunlight streaming through the drapes. I jump up. Why didn't Sarah wake me? I throw on a clean day dress and apron, gather my unruly hair in a rough ribbon and race down the stairs. Breakfast has been cleared? I race back upstairs, following the sound of voices to the trunk room, finding Mama and Harry there already. Without me.

'Oh, how are you feeling, hinny?' says Ma. I frown at her, as obviously I'm *feeling* outraged that no one woke me. 'Sarah said you weren't well in your stomach and asked to miss breakfast.'

'Sarah! That little . . .' Harry's eyebrows rise at my tone so I bite my lip and remember what I said to good quiet Sarah: *you're so boring you make me sick.*

So she told Ma I *was* sick.

I have to give it to her, it's a mighty fine way to get me back.

If only I didn't sleep so heavily. Ma always says I switch on and off like a light bulb.

'I'm quite well now, Mama,' I say sweetly. 'So, Harry, how long were you in Sydney? Did you see a crocodile?'

But she closes the trunk and Harry looks at his pocket watch. He lays a kind hand on my shoulder.

'Tell you what, I'll write all about all the animals I've ever seen on my travels in a letter just for you, and I should be able to duck in again in the summer. But right now, I'm afraid my ship awaits.'

I raise my chin, biting back tears, determined he won't catch a glimpse of even one.

'You've just got time to see the horses with Frankie, Harold. And you, Clara, there's porridge on the stove when you are ready. Or take yourself back to bed, you're looking quite pale.'

With that, Harry and Ma leave me in the trunk room, their chatter and footsteps echoing down the hall and then the stairs. Not a thought for me. Silly baby Clarty with her funny questions.

I grind away hot tears with my fists, then through the blur the trunk comes into focus. The house is now quiet. The trunk is huge. I twist the key in the lock and it springs open to reveal a tartan blanket. Gramma died a year ago and these are some of her clothes, cutlery, fine linens, china ornaments carefully wrapped, hand-crocheted shawls and blankets, candlesticks, papers and books. This is Harry's mother's share of Grandmama's belongings, packed ready to go back to Mama's sister in England. A scent of lavender and camphor drifts up from inside the trunk. I shake my head and wipe my nose. I don't want to think about Gramma right now, I still miss her. At least she had seen how good I was with animals. She had trusted me.

I can't stop staring at the trunk. I'm small for twelve and that's usually annoying. But I'd easily fit inside the huge chest.

I could lie on the blanket and just close the lid. I'd simply disappear. That would make them care, wouldn't it?

When the front door swings, and the sound of my brothers laughing with Harry floats up the stairs, my decision is made.

I lift items out of the trunk carefully and stow them in another empty trunk. All that's left is some sheets at the bottom, two tartan blankets and one of Gramma's shawls.

I climb inside the trunk.

Some of the other trunks are flimsy board, but this is hardwood. I reach up and lower the lid. The light narrows to a crack, the darkness only broken by slivers of light slicing through the joins of the wooden slats. There's definitely enough air to be able to breathe and I feel safe lying on Gramma's things, enclosed in her cosy smell of fresh baked bread and hay. I can't stretch out, but also I'm not curled in so tight a ball it's uncomfortable. I lie on my side with my knees only halfway bent, then yawn and pull Gramma's crochet shawl over me. Just like when I was a little girl, snuggled on her terrace settle for an afternoon nap. I rest my hands under my head and my eyes droop, heavy.

Let them search for me for the rest of the day, I've had it with the lot of them.

Thursday
11th
April
1912

11TH APRIL
FROM: TITANIC
TO: NEW YORK

HELLO BOY. DINING WITH YOU TONIGHT
IN SPIRIT, HEART WITH YOU ALWAYS.
BEST LOVE, GIRL

Gramma's chair rocks, I'm safe and warm, on her lap, back and forth, back and forth . . .

I blink awake into darkness, my arm flailing out, knuckles hitting something hard, a solid surface at my feet . . . the trunk. I huff out a breath in relief. My head is heavy.

Why aren't my eyes getting used to the dark? The slices of light are gone. And it's so . . . noisy.

Suddenly I'm wide awake.

The rocking wasn't just a dream, the trunk really is moving. I push on the lid, but it doesn't budge. I ram it with the palms of both hands, pressing my back into the sheets and blankets beneath me, mind whirling with images of the catch. I left the hinge tilted up, I know I did.

My breath comes in little gasps. How long have I been asleep?

'Help! I'm in here, help!'

The darned lock needs to open. Someone needs to hear me. Now.

I force myself to calm down by imagining Ma sniffing her smelling salts, and drawing deep breaths through my nose. I need to gather my wits and figure out what is going on outside. The cracks on the top of the trunk let light through when I lay down, but now must be covered by something sitting on top of it. I can't make out voices, just a trundling roar. Could that be the cart, or have I already been loaded on to a train?

That thought sets me off yelling again. I shriek and pound against the side of the trunk until my voice breaks. But finally I cover my own mouth, forcing myself to stop. They won't be able to hear me if I am on the cart or the train. I try to imagine what could be going on outside the trunk. I'm piled in among the luggage so need to save my voice for when I have a chance of being heard. I shift the blanket and fabrics from one corner so I can almost sit with my head bent. Then I stretch out fully. If I lie in a strange diagonal with my head in a top corner and my feet burrowed in the opposite bottom corner, I can almost straighten my legs. I'm not stiff, so I can't have been in here that long.

When we reach wherever we are going I'll be sure to make them hear me. They'll hear me in Australia! I almost smile at the thought, pleased I've calmed myself down enough now to think. It's only half an hour on the cart to Montgomery station, then an hour on the train through New York to the harbour. Would it be so bad if I was already on the train? I put both hands around behind my head and manage to cross my legs. None of my six older brothers and sisters have pulled a stunt like this before.

I'm on the train, must be; the cart would rock more and I'd hear the clopping of hooves, rather than this low roar. It's strange to think of me sleeping as I was lifted down the stairs and on and off the cart, then into the train. Why didn't they notice it was too heavy? I suppose all the vases and books I took out weighed a lot.

Maybe I'll even see RMS *Carpathia* before Harry puts me on the train back to Montgomery. Imagine that! My brothers will be livid with jealousy. I am lost in fantasy when my suspicions are confirmed with a hoot of the whistle, a jerking stop and finally the hiss of steam. I scrabble up into an almost upright seated position and clear my throat.

'Help! Here – in the trunk!'

But it is so loud out there. More swooshing steam, voices, banging nearby, a bell, a dog barking. When the trunk tips then slams down, I crack my elbow against the wood. I'm shaken into silence. What is happening now? Whatever it is, I don't want to be crushed half to death. I roll myself in the blankets as the trunk tips again. Now my cries are too muffled, but I need the blanket over my head – what if they tip the trunk upside down? I'll be knocked out or bruised half to death.

A metallic sound clicks against the wood by my head, making me think of chains.

'Harry! Harold Cottam!' I call. 'I'm in the trunk. Help!'

I slip my first and little finger in my mouth and whistle as loudly as I can, but coming from inside the trunk, wrapped in blankets, the sound is too faint to be heard.

I peep out to see light seeping through the joins in the trunk but before I can feel relief, the splinters of light are cut by lines. Chains wrapping the trunk. Bands of darkness. Then movement, different movement, the trunk ...lifts.

A horn sounds, a fishy smell oozes into the trunk.

The docks. The train led right to the docks.

My stomach swoops. The trunk is swinging.

The crate I'm inside is in the air, swaying like the

pendulum in a grandfather clock.

Bracing my feet and my hands on either end, I stop myself from sliding around, barely able to breathe let alone scream. I'm still wrapped in the blanket, now sweating.

And more swinging movement – upwards or maybe down. Another horn. I try to picture what is happening outside: trunks and other luggage being hoisted through the air on one of those cranes. I wriggle my head out of the blanket and scrabble to uncover the base of the trunk.

Light is now shining through the bottom slats.

There is nothing below me. My stomach rises into my throat.

What if the chain slips or breaks? I'll land in the harbour and water will trickle into the trunk, slowly filling it up. No one will hear my cries.

I'll be trapped in here. I'll sink.

I'll drown.

This time I have no words or even cries for help.

I scream and scream.

The swing through the air in the trunk dizzies me. I'm too hot and terrified of that fatal drop, the water dribbling in . . . I'm suddenly sure I'm going to be sick. I can't vomit in here, I don't know how long I'm going to be trapped. I pant and whimper, eyes squeezed tight, legs and arms trembling where I'm still braced to stop myself slamming into the wood.

I sway until I feel so awful I almost wish the crane would drop me.

Finally I land with a jolt.

Not a splash.

I stretch my arms and legs in relief, choking back the urge to be sick. I press my face against the widest crack; I can barely get my fingernails into it, let alone see anything, but I can suck fresh air if I sip against it. This break from terror barely lasts a moment before the trunk is moved again.

I call out, but my voice is now gruff and faint from screaming. The trunk tips lengthways and starts to move again, shifting me so I land with a violent thud and roll into a ball, covering my head. Once again we are moving and I try to thump the sides of the trunk as best I can. Thankfully this part of my doomed journey is short. I land with a clump; the trunk shifts along the floor and is still. More thumps, other trunks? There's voices again, already fading when I call out then whistle once more.

Hear me, please hear me.

The light is dimmer here – I sense the trunk is inside somewhere – then all at once complete darkness.

Someone has closed a door on me.

6

I've tried to think this through without working myself into a state, and there really aren't that many options.

I must be in the luggage hold of RMS *Carpathia*.

Locked in a trunk.

On the bright side, I haven't tumbled into the harbour, I'm not hurt, and the sick feeling has faded.

Now to get out of this dratted trunk before the ship sets sail.

There must be a way. I untangle the blankets from where they have become twisted around me and lie back on the lumpy pile. Lucky I had them or I'd be black and blue. I breathe and the fear sweat cools me down. The trunk seemed surprisingly large when I climbed into it, but thoughts of coffins now spring to mind. I regret sneaking reads of my brother's penny dreadfuls now.

Be sensible about this. Someone will be down here soon, they have to be. But sinister thoughts pile up. What if they never come down here once the ship is sailing? Harry said they were going to Trieste. How long would it take to get to Trieste? Where even is it? Definitely somewhere in Europe. If only I'd found out more about RMS *Carpathia*. Harry said she was a reliable ship but not the biggest or fastest . . .

How long until I thirst to death?

My throat is already dry and sore from all the screaming and my head pounds. I'll make it worse by panicking, I could actually make myself die quicker . . .

Distraction. I'll find out exactly what is in the trunk with me.

I squeeze into one corner of the trunk while I rake around among the blankets and linens until my fingers touch something cool and smooth. It can't be. There can't be a bottle of water in here, I've got to be imagining this.

'Yes!' I hiss, feeling the bottle with both hands in the dark. It's real! I press the glass against my cheek then uncork the top and take a tiny sip.

The sugar hits me and I feel a burst of energy and relief. Maple syrup. Of course Mama would put a bottle in for Aunt Orla.

I need to save it; I don't know how long I will be in here.

My relief melts away with the taste of the syrup. The stickiness coats my mouth. I hear Mama's voice now, telling me to go easy on the cordial: 'If it's too sweet it won't do 'aught for your thirst.'

Syrup isn't water. I've helped make it, seen the water boiled off in the huge vats. The excitement of finding it drops away with the bottom of my stomach.

Could I smash the bottle and use it to try to break the lock? With a sliver of glass I could prise it ...

I would cut myself and the syrup would go every-where. But – better than thirsting to death. I'll shelve that plan for if I get even more desperate.

I make myself concentrate. I was finding out exactly what is inside the trunk with me. I feel two thick wool blankets, then what feels like a lace-edged tablecloth. I can imagine it, one Gramma embroidered the edges of herself. Then some sheets and pillowcases, again with embroidery. A fine shawl, crocheted in wool. Gramma always wore one. I keep it aside to wrap around me if I get cold. Now I'm at the base of the trunk. So far, nothing that is going to help me get out. I run my hands over the entire base of wood, into the far corners and back towards me, then shuffle around to make sure I haven't missed anything where I'm crouched. My hand hits cold metal, and I know what it is even before my fingers confirm it.

A hoof pick.

Now this is a bit more like it.

I explore the heavy shape; it is definitely one of Gramma's old hoof picks. I bring it out in front of my face and smell the iron. I've seen these being forged by the farrier in sprays of sparks. A long rod of iron, around the thickness of my little finger, hammered into a loop at one end as a handle and bashed into a sharp hook at the other. It was Gramma who taught me how to look after my horse's feet, using a hoof pick to hook out stones and clean out dried mud. Mama said I was too young, but Gramma argued if I was old enough to ride, I was old enough to tend my horse.

I run my finger over the sharp point of the hook and smile into the darkness. I am getting out of here.

At that moment the horn of the ship sounds, filling my ears, the low hum of it vibrating through the trunk into my bones.

Is the *Carpathia* really readying to set sail? I don't have any time to spare.

But I can't even locate the lock in the complete

darkness. I sigh. Why is everything about this so difficult? I manoeuvre so I'm in the middle of the trunk where I think I remember the latch was positioned, finding the join of the lid with my fingertips. I prise the hook of the hoof pick into the tiny gap in the wood and start to ease splinters out, finding that beneath the layer of varnish, the wood is softer.

I work hard and quickly, and am soon sweating again. I wipe my forehead on my wrist and keep on – hack, hack, hack – clearing the shards of wood away with my other hand. Same again. And again. I've definitely got splinters in my fingers now, but I keep on.

A weird noise.

I stop. Nothing. I shake my head; must have imagined it, because it sounded like a growl. Probably a creak from the ship's timbers, showing we are about to leave. It's a sign to set to work more quickly, increasing to five hits of the hook before clearing, feeling the wood.

But when I stop to shake out my trembling arm, the sound is there again, clear. And close. Very close indeed.

Definitely a growl. Goosebumps rise on my arms.

A deep rumbling snarl comes from directly outside the trunk.

UNITED STATES SENATE INQUIRY

Day 9 - 27th April 1912
Testimony of Sidney Daniels

SENATOR BOURNE: Tell me about the time running up to the sinking, including dates and times where you can. What happened after you set sail for Queenstown in Ireland?

- That would have been the 11th of April, sir. We'd already picked up the passengers from Cherbourg in France and then went to Queenstown, leaving there on the 11th.

SENATOR BOURNE: Very good. So your duties as a steward were underway?

- Yes, sir. It was down to work. We had a routine, swabbing the cabins, changing sheets where needed; our third-class sections were large so most of the day was taken up by it, sir.

SENATOR BOURNE: Did you go up on deck?

- Yes, sir, in the little time we had after our shift and dinner.

SENATOR BOURNE: And did the third-class stewards mostly keep to themselves, or did you speak to other crew members during your recreational time?

- Mostly to ourselves, there wasn't much time to be getting to know others. But on the 11th I did talk to the lookout Freddie Fleet up on deck.

SENATOR BOURNE: I'd like to hear that entire conversation with Mr Fleet please, Mr Daniels. I will not interrupt.

- I was taking a few minutes of fresh air on deck, looking up, wondering why one of the funnels had no smoke coming out of it. Must have been standing there with my mouth hanging open, because this young sailor asked if I was catching flies. I laughed and he told me the fourth funnel of Titanic was part of the ventilation system so it would never have smoke coming out of it. The only reason it was so tall was to fit in with the others and to make the ship look even more majestic.

I guessed that the other funnels were that high so that the soot and smoke from the engines did not bother the passengers on deck. He seemed impressed and even asked me whether I was going to be a seaman when I was older. That's when he introduced himself as Freddie Fleet, one of the ship's lookouts. I was a bit in awe then, to be honest, sir. I'd thought he was just one of the able seamen, he seemed awful young for such a job.

SENATOR BOURNE: Anything else you can recall from that exchange? Take your time.

- Well, he pointed out the crow's nest up on the foremast and told me it was dreadful cold up there, and showed me the chilblains on his hands. I told him I wished I'd brought some of my ma's liniment with me, then . . . I felt a bit daft because not exactly helpful, was it?

SENATOR BOURNE: Did Mr Fleet talk to you about any of the equipment he used when he was on lookout?

- No, sir. He just said it looked a smooth crossing and we'd make good time. Then he bid me goodnight.

SENATOR BOURNE: And how did Mr Fleet seem to you. His attitude to his work?

- I couldn't say, sir. He was just a friendly chap. I suppose he seemed . . . proud of what he did.

I stop hacking at the seam between the trunk and its lid and sit stock-still, listening, the iron hoof pick hot and slick in my hand.

How can it be a growl? I'm hearing things now. All this sitting crunched up in the dark is turning me into a 'fraidy cat.

Another growl, low and deep, very close. There's no mistaking it, especially as it's followed by a sniff, right where I've been attacking the wood with my hook. I thought my mouth was already as dry as it could get, but I was wrong.

The next rolling thunder of a growl brings a picture of snarling teeth to mind.

What animal growls like that?

A big one.

All is quiet again. Can I hear panting or is that my blood rushing in my ears?

I reach out the hoof pick and tap gently at the wood. More rumbling, now sniffing, and then a clicking – the sound of claws hitting the floor. It is pacing away, then back, away then back. Another growl.

My mind jumps around like a frog in springtime. How do animals get to zoos? They must travel by boat, in crates or cages in the hold. One could have escaped . . . could be a lion, or a bear . . .

But animals need food and water, so at least someone will definitely come down here sooner or later, won't they?

The horn sounds again and then movement below me, another growl from the animal and then the slightest of shifts, a new vibration through the floor of the trunk. The engine. The engine is fired up.

The steamship *Carpathia* is setting sail.

My breath comes quick. I can't be trapped in the hold of a steamer to Europe, with an escaped beast.

For a moment I allow myself to curl up in the dark, hearing more growling at my movement. I need to carry on working at the wood, hacking and hoping to hit the lock even if the animal out there is going to kill me. I can't die of thirst, and I'm going to get weaker if I wait too long. My head spins and I press my face into Gramma's shawl and release a little sob. Well, there's no one here to see, is there?

I let frustration wash over me, tears soaking into the wooden shawl. I could do with one of Ma's hugs now. Why didn't she come looking for me? If I'd just made it up with her . . .

'I can't do this any more, I don't like it, I didn't mean to. Please . . . it's not *fair*!'

I deliberately sob louder than the animal's growls so I can't hear them, until I'm cried out, exhausted. Then somehow, I fall asleep.

I stretch and yelp as my elbow thumps wood, followed by my toes.

Memories speed back in. No growling. Did I dream it?

My hip aches, my back is twisted. Is it night, or day? No sound but the rumble of RMS *Carpathia*, which must now be at sea.

I scrabble for the maple syrup bottle and the hoof pick. I'm that thirsty I take a gulp of the syrup and can't even enjoy the sweetness as it immediately glues my mouth up. Right away I hear that sniffing again. No growls this time, just sniffing at the crack I was working at with the hoof pick.

Whatever the animal is, it's been sleeping right outside the trunk.

I sit up.

A tiny growl is followed by a whine.

Hungry? It was the smell of the sweet syrup that woke it. My mind forms a picture of a bear, tearing at meat.

No. This could be good, this has to be good. If this beast likes the syrup more than it likes me, it will be distracted if I open the lid and throw the syrup at it. Even if it is a lion, tiger, bear ... If I take it by surprise and use a syrup diversion, I might have a chance to escape.

I have a plan.

When I pick at the splintered wood with my tool there's a loud growl.

I uncork the syrup bottle and hold it against the crack.

'The sound of me scrabbling around in here scares you, does it? But smell the nice syrup,' I whisper to myself.

A wheedling sort of whimper.

There's no point in waiting for the animal's keeper to come and give it dinner. I might *be* the dinner by the time that happens. I try to smile at my own joke.

I set to the wood again with the metal hook. More

snarling, but I can't listen, I need to concentrate on the plan.

Suddenly my efforts are accompanied by a scrape and scratch plus whining. The animal outside – I can't help but imagine it is a bear – is trying to get into the trunk at the same time I'm trying to get out. I stop for a moment, rubbing my wrist and panting. It's unnerving to have a big beast trying to get at me – *at the syrup, not me, the syrup* – but is it a bad thing if it gets me out of here quicker?

I listen to the scraping, my ear to the splintered pit I've made. Sometimes the claws are against metal, sometimes against wood. The lock. I can tell where the lock is from the screeching sound the claws make when they hit it. I get back to work directly behind it, whittling the hook into the wood until finally it screeches across metal.

I can't help a little whoop of delight, which sets off a volley of growls and more frantic scratching against the wood. The crate shakes.

Please let someone hear the animal making this noise and come to my rescue.

I sigh. I can't wait for that to happen.

I can now lever out chunks of wood using the metal of the lock – a brass box embedded in the wood – to help. The grind of my iron hook prying around the edge of the brass lock sets my teeth on edge but I finally break right through the wood. A yelp from the other side as I push against the lid above me and it moves a little. The wood is splintered enough, it's loose around the lock.

It's going to come free. I laugh in triumph. The beast snarls.

I'm getting out, but whatever it is outside is getting in.

Could I lie down and kick the lid off? I'd be lying on my back like a helpless beetle. Like dinner on a platter. No, I need to be ready to spring – throw the maple syrup bottle and get to safety.

Perhaps it's best not to think too much.

I shove all of the fabrics out of the way into a corner so my feet are wedged against the base of the trunk. Curled over, I duck my head forward and brace my shoulders against the lid.

My stomach churns and my heart batters my chest like it too is trapped in a trunk. Well here goes.

One. Two. Three—

I ram my shoulders up, the lid springs open as the lock busts free from the wood, and I burst out, throwing the syrup bottle high and long and hearing the clatter as it lands. A skitter of claws and a huge black shadow. I spring out of the trunk, immediately toppling over on top of another trunk, my legs stiff and useless. I struggle to my feet, gulping in the space, the air, so jazzed to be outside the box.

No time for that now. It isn't pitch-black; I can just make out I am in a large area piled with luggage, crates and trunks. I scramble up on top of a chest and then on to a wooden crate. Now I am high up and safe for a moment, my eyes can adjust to the dark. The hold is not full and across a space of empty floor I spot the animal. It is huge, shaggy and black, its back to me, slurping and grinding its teeth against the glass, the bottle rolling around the floor batted by giant paws.

I gasp. The size of it.

It really is a bear.

8

What are the chances of being locked in a trunk and ending up on a ship, let alone being trapped in the hold with a bear?

I can hear Frank now. 'That's our Clara, up to her usual antics.'

Can bears climb? I reckon I'm safe up here on the piled trunks, for a minute at least.

With the bear busy with the syrup bottle, I stretch my legs out and survey the hold of the *Carpathia*. In the far corner a flight of wooden stairs leads to a door – that's where I need to be. Trouble is, that's where the bear is too, chasing the bottle of syrup around the floor by the bottom step. Anything else I can use? I squint around but it doesn't look good. It isn't pitch-dark, so light must be getting in somehow and that seems to be from behind another pile of crates. I trust my legs a bit more now. The animal is still busy, so I make my way down on to a case, climb on top of the mass of crates, lie on my stomach and peer over to where the light seems to be coming from.

A porthole!

I check on the bear – hard at work on the syrup – and climb down behind the crates to gaze out of the round window. The ship is slicing through the water and the horizon stretches as far as I can see, no sign of land. Streaks of pink cloud. Sunset. The sea is only around three feet below me and I stare out at it in wonder, watching the foam scud away from the ship. I forget my situation for a moment, feeling a twinge of excitement as I press my hands against the glass. This is the biggest adventure I've ever had. But I can't stay down here. I need to get up those stairs.

I'm startled by a new sound, a creak, a change in the light – someone here, someone is coming. But I can't climb back up the wall of crates, I need to go round . . .

'Help! I'm here, help me!' I yell, but my voice cracks and then a slam. Has someone come and gone that quickly?

I run to where I can climb back over the wall of packing cases.

The bear has gone. Or is it hiding? I creep out and almost immediately hear the door open again. The growling is so loud that although I can hear a man's frustrated voice, I can't make out what he's saying, and as I call out the door is slammed shut again.

Darn it, darn it, darn it!

I had my chance and missed it.

The bear is now at the base of the stairs, head in a wooden bucket. I see in the half-light that the bottle of syrup has rolled towards me. I need to be quick – by the snuffling sounds the animal is making, it won't take long to eat its supper and it will be back at that syrup.

With a deep breath I clamber down the crates, heart thumping. The bottle is resting in a corner just a few steps away. I slip down to the floor, grimacing at the creak as the case I was standing on pings back into shape. My eyes cling to the black shape of the bear, head still burrowed in the bucket, but also note the maple syrup bottle which – with a slight tilt of the ship – is now rolling away from me. This is my only chance: if I throw it to the far end behind some cases and the animal goes after it, my route to the stairs will be clear.

I've got to take the risk.

Diving across the floor to grab the bottle, I huff out

when my fingers close around the sticky glass. Got you. Then I scramble up at the same time the bear's head pops up from the bucket.

Black eyes glisten in the gloom, a pink tongue hangs out. We watch each other for a moment that drags on for ever and with that huge bushy head and glossy snout, it really is a bear. Throw the bottle and escape up those stairs . . .

I fling the bottle across the hold. Except . . . nothing happens. In a second I see the bottle is mainly empty now, so very light and sticky.

So sticky, it is stuck firm to the palm of my hand.

Blast it!

Now the gigantic shaggy mass of black fur and clicking claws is coming at me, and I'm too slow, I'm too far from the cases to climb in time, and the last thing I want to do is turn my back on it, but I don't have a choice.

The beast thinks I've stolen its treat!

I try to scramble up the cases one-handed but the animal grabs my skirt and growls, shaking me from side to side. I lose my footing, tumble back so I'm on my back in exactly the worst place I could be, syrup bottle stuck fast to my hand, the animal above me, steamy breath on my face. I close my eyes tight, curling, covering my face, braced for ripping claws and biting teeth.

Soft, rough, wet.

No teeth, no claws, not the slightest growl.

It's licking my hand that holds the syrup bottle. I peer out from under my arms. The fur is soft. The smell is musty and warm. No bared teeth, just ears, drooly chops and whiskers.

The bear is not a bear.

It is the biggest, shaggiest, blackest monster of a dog I've ever seen.

But that's what it is. A dog.

It's a *dog*. A huge, slobbering dog.

The bear dog's black eyes are half closed in pleasure as it licks my hand still holding the syrup bottle. I shuffle backwards until I hit a crate and then sit up, all the while tensing my arm to make sure the animal can get at the syrup.

My instinct is slow to catch up on the new information and I fight the urge to snatch my arm away and run.

But with any dog, running means chasing.

It might not be a bear, and it looks kind of dopey now I'm real close, but I don't know it's friendly. I need to be smart about this.

The licking of the dog has released the sticky bottle's hold on my hand. I put it down in front of me. Bear Dog grips the bottle between its two paws and licks contentedly, reminding me so much of Peg back home when she is given a bone, that I start to relax. I stand slowly. The dog looks up, without a break in licking. Well, things are a lot better than they were. Even if Bear Dog doesn't turn out to be friendly, he also isn't an actual bear.

Someone is coming down here to feed him and take him up on deck, surely once a day at least, so I'm not going to be trapped down here for too much longer. My shoulders slump. Not too much longer is still far too long when you are as thirsty as I am.

Bear Dog must have heard my sigh because he releases the bottle in front of him and also sighs.

Just a dog.

I warily reach out my closed fist to him. He sniffs, then gives it a wet-nosed nudge. His black plume of a tail lifts and wags, and when he stands, I gasp. His head is halfway between my waist and armpit! I remember the book on the shelf back at the farmhouse among the farming manuals. Aunt Orla sent it to us for Christmas when I was small. *Our Dogs and All about Them*, that was it! I used to love looking at the plates, and Frank would read it to me. Everyone laughed because they thought I should be listening to *Peter Pan* or *Rebecca of Sunnybrook Farm*, but I was only interested if a book contained animals. I try to recall the photos. What was the biggest dog? The St Bernard with its brandy cask around its neck. I remember a story in the newspaper Papa showed me. There was a picture, two of those dogs digging a person out of the snow. But those weren't black . . .

I know! The fishing dogs from Canada.

'Are you a Newfoundland? Is that what you are, boy?' I say.

He wags again and I reach below his ear and give his fur a ruffle. Bear Dog leans into my hand. I remember his growling at the trunk when I was inside. It was an understandable reaction from his point of view. Probably hasn't come across many small girls locked in wooden boxes trying to get out. Poor hound.

'I scared you, did I? You big softy,' I say. He must belong to someone. I ruffle under his chin then search beneath his black mane and find a leather collar. I follow it around to a brass tag, keeping an eye on that wagging tail, ready to stop if the huge animal shows any sign he doesn't like what I'm doing.

I can just about make out the tag, engraved. Rigel. What a strange name; I don't even know how you say it.

'Is it like . . . Wriggle?' I say. 'Is that you?'

The dog gives a soft snort.

'Or is it Ree-gal, like a king?'

He watches me as if waiting.

'Guess not then. What about Rye-jel?' The dog wags his tail so hard his whole back end dances from side to side. That must be it.

'Good boy, Rigel,' I say.

With the discovery of the collar I relax further and decide to try something.

'Sit.' Rigel sits.

'Stay,' I say, and walk to the stairs. Rigel whines a little, but stays where he is. I come back and ruffle under his ears and he licks my nose.

He's a pet or a working dog. A good dog. So why is he locked up down here, all on his own?

Finally he trots over to the stairs to give the bucket a last lick. I follow, and head up the stairs to the door, drawing in a deep breath. I turn the knob. Locked. Rigel is behind me and barks.

I bang on the door with the flat of my hand. I call out, then whistle. Rigel releases a whole volley of barks. Anyone out there won't hear me calling with him woofing like that.

I try some more commands, but he clearly doesn't understand 'quiet' or 'shush'. The tiny amount of light coming from the portholes behind the crates is dimming so it is almost pitch-black again.

Night. If they only come to him once a day — I need water.

'What is it, Rigel?' I say.

The dog sniffs at something and I run back down the stairs, wishing my mouth weren't so dry and my head didn't feel like a small blacksmith was banging the inside of it with a mallet.

It is getting too dark; soon I won't be able to see anything at all.

I follow the dog into a shadowed corner. Beneath the stairs are huge barrels. I blink. On the side of one is a tap. It can't be.

I twist the tap and water flows out. Clever dog! I kneel down and catch it in my mouth, gulping and giggling as it splashes over my face. Rigel licks at the floor and at my neck. I laugh again and finally turn off the tap, not caring that my skirt, blouse and apron are soaked. My stomach slops and relief swamps me like the drink has swamped my insides. I drag over the empty food bucket and slosh in some water for Rigel to lap at, but that's not what he really wants. He is now sniffing at one of the smaller crates stored near the barrels. I investigate as he stands on his back legs snuffling.

'You want me to open this one, boy?' I say. 'What's in there?'

The hoof pick easily prises open the lid and I gasp as I make out the contents. Cookies. Piles and piles of cookies, wrapped in paper. I think of Ma's butter shortbread, fresh from the oven, and my mouth waters. I inspect one; doesn't look much like shortbread, more like the ginger squares Gramma used to make, but I'm not complaining. I pass one to Bear Dog – after all, he was the one who found them – before biting down. I almost snap my teeth. So hard! Bear Dog is crunching away but I can only gnaw off a little corner at a time. It isn't even sweet – plain and slightly salty – but I'm that hungry my disappointment doesn't last long. I grab a handful and sit as I break into them.

At last the worst of my hunger pangs have gone and the hold is almost completely dark. I shiver. It's got colder with night falling and my wet skirt and blouse cling. I make my way in the thick gloom to Gramma's trunk, wrap up in her shawl, grab out the blankets and sheets, arranging them in a rough bed of sorts, and lie down beside the trunk, eyelids drooping, still cold, until I feel warmth pressing at my back. Bear Dog. Rigel.

I roll over, curl into the fur of his belly and soon fall fast asleep.

11TH APRIL
FROM: TITANIC
TO: CAPE RACE MRS MILLING IN
DENMARK

I AM VERY WELL. CALM WEATHER.
WONDERFUL SHIP. I AM ENJOYING
MYSELF. JACOB

Friday
12th
April
1912

'What the blazes?'

I startle awake to a man's narrow face with a tiny, pointed nose looming over me.

'A stowaway, is it?'

I sit up, looking for Rigel. The dog is behind the man, softly growling.

The man is older, wearing a navy uniform with a grey apron over the top, and despite him seeming rather unfriendly, I smile. Finally I'm going to get free. But the man doesn't give me a chance to speak.

'And a girl at that? Well I never. It's straight to the

captain with you. Planning a pickpocketing spree in the first-class cabins no doubt.' He stops, glaring at the trunk I had been asleep in front of. 'You've been at the luggage already, you little scoundrel!'

'I certainly have not!' I say, indignant. 'Please, you've got this all wrong. I am related to—'

'I couldn't care less if you are the daughter of the Queen of Sheba.' The man reaches out as if to grab my ear and then whips his hand back when a warning growl rumbles from Rigel. 'Trust you to be making friends with a filthy little urchin. Like attracts like,' says the man. 'I'm not scared of you, mutt.'

The man clearly is scared as he has come prepared and waves a huge steel ladle at the dog, who whines then barks.

He swipes again at my ear, brushing past as I scramble to my feet and duck away.

'Get your meat hooks off me, I'm coming, all right!' I say. 'My cousin is Harry Cottam. And I'd like to know who *you* are!'

'The insolence of it! I am Mr Greeve-Birtwistle, Chief Steward First Class, not that it's any of your concern. I'll not have another word from you, save it for the captain,' snaps the man as he waves me to the stairs in front of him. Rigel bares his teeth and as we start up the stairs he snaps at the steward's heels. The man whips around, swinging the metal ladle far too close to the dog's head.

'Don't you dare hit him!' I yell, grabbing the steward's arm. 'You can't just go around striking animals and manhandling people. Who have ended up on your boat quite by accident, I might add.'

'A likely story!' says the man, shaking me off. With another threatening wave of the ladle he slams the door on the barking dog and herds me along a passageway.

I walk briskly to keep a gap between myself and that ladle. 'I am the cousin of Harold Cottam,' I say in my best voice, copying the one Mama uses when talking to the pastor.

'And why would our wireless operator's cousin be hiding in the hold, pray tell?'

I pause. Where to start? I hid inside a trunk back at my family ranch because I was in a bad mood? Heat rises in my face.

'It was an accident, all right? There's no need to treat me so . . . rudely!'

There's a scraping behind us, the click of claws against metal. I hear the steward gasp and realize I didn't see him lock the door – he was too busy being furious with me for no good reason. A burst of scrabbling and I turn to see that giant shiny wet nose nudge open the door, and Rigel is free and bounding towards us.

The steward bellows, 'Stop him!'

But even if I wanted to, I couldn't. That great black thundercloud of a dog gallops past us and down the ship's corridor, leaving swirling air and a scent of musty dog and maple syrup.

11

'After him!'

Mr Greeve-Birt – whatever his name is, the steward – continues to bellow out commands, but I leave him far behind me as I race after Rigel, that bear of a dog, around the corner of a corridor and up two flights of stairs. You'd think I'd catch the huge fellow on the stairs, but he's bounding three at a time and I don't have a chance. We must be in the passengers' section of the steam liner now; the walls are panelled and the floor tiled.

Voices and other sounds come from behind a glass-paned door and Rigel makes a turn, claws screeching across the tiles just as the door opens and a man in a bowler hat strides out, gasps and covers his head.

'Sorry!'

I don't know why I'm suddenly responsible for the rampaging dog, but Rigel and I seem to be in this together.

I swing around the door and into the ship's barber salon where two men perch on leather chairs as the dog gallops circles around them, spinning their seats, hair flying everywhere.

There's no stopping Rigel now. I've seen this with young horses and with Peg. If you wind them up enough, they need to unwind again. This dog had been locked up for too long.

'Oh, my giddy aunt!' The barber is sitting on a counter-top, gripping a small comb like a sword.

Finally Rigel slows and I step in front of him, hands raised. 'There you are now, calm down now, Rigel,' I say in the croon I use for Folly. 'We should probably get you on a leash.'

Rigel stops in front of me.

The barber jumps down from the counter, loosens his tie and hands it to me. 'This your dog, kid?' he says in a broad Brooklyn accent.

'No! He escaped from the hold,' I say, and then we both look down at Rigel. The hair he was running through is bright orange and is now stuck around his mouth. It looks like the giant black dog now has a set of luxurious ginger whiskers.

The barber and I laugh at the same time. The men in the chairs don't seem to find it so amusing.

I fasten the barber's necktie around Rigel's collar.

The barber offers his fist to Rigel, who licks it and wags his tail.

'No harm done. Just a daft hound,' says the barber. He brandishes a comb and with the help of his spray bottle, manages to brush out Rigel's new hairstyle and even snip away a few knots. The dog shuts his eyes as if he actually likes it! I find myself grinning as I watch the barber work and catch my breath.

Rigel might be a bit of a wild one, but he's also a very good dog.

'I've never seen the like of it,' says one of the two passengers still in the barber chairs.

'Are we in a pooches' parlour? Absolute disgrace,' says the other, snatching the towel around his neck and throwing it to the floor before he storms out.

The steward finally bursts in. When he sees Rigel being groomed, he gulps in breaths, hands on his knees.

'Oh, I might have known you were supposed to be in charge of this splendid chap, Mister Grave-Birtwhimper,' says the barber, eyes twinkling.

'It's Greeve-Birtwistle as you full well know, Chan. If you can't say it, then Greeve is fine.'

'Ah, but then we'd be getting you all mixed up with that fine officer son of yours.'

The two men glare at each other.

'This mutt is going straight back to the hold. I'll ask you to escort him, Chan. I need to deliver this child to the captain.'

'Pooch can wait here, but I'm taking him nowhere. Anyway, don't know why you're blowing your wig,' says the barber, 'seems to me this little miss is your heroine – fellow here would still be tearing the place up if it weren't for her.'

'Well, that shows what little you know,' huffs Mr Greeve-Birtwistle, 'because this *little miss* is a thieving stowaway.'

I hand the necktie leash attached to the giant mischief-maker of a dog to the barber, Mr Chan.

'I'm Clara Scott, and this is Rigel,' I say, 'and I'm not a thief.'

'Rigel is it?' says Mr Chan, seemingly not worried if I am or not, as he combs through the fur under Rigel's chin with his fingers. 'I know a superb tailor called Nigel but I've never heard of a Rigel.'

'Me neither,' I say.

'This is quite enough—'

'Mr Grave-Beetwinkle. I almost forgot you were

there,' says Mr Chan and winks at me.

'I'm coming, all right?' I say. 'I need to contact my cousin, but if you don't want Rigel with us then you are going to have to wait a moment.'

The first class steward's pointed nose turns very red and very shiny, but he nods, and uses a handkerchief to polish his buttons.

'Rigel, sit.'

The dog sits.

'Rigel, stay,' I say.

The dog looks at me and then at Mr Chan and gives a tiny whine but doesn't move.

'Good boy, wait there.'

Mr Greeve-Birtwistle glares. Mr Chan looks at me in wonder, like I'm doing some sort of magic, but it isn't anything special. Rigel just knows the same commands we use with Peg. But I suppose not everyone was raised on a farm.

I ask the steward if the dog has an owner – but he just snaps that it's none of my concern and ushers me out of the door, forcing me to walk in front of him as if I'm going to run off.

We stride down a long corridor, with plain wood panelling and many doors – whether they are for passengers or crew I can't tell with Greeve-Birtwistle nipping at my heels. Then up a flight of stairs, never once seeing a glimpse of natural light. Same again on a brighter white-panelled corridor; this one I'm sure is for the higher-class passengers as it's lost that metallic musty smell of further down. Double doors swing open, and inside I see a spacious dining room, with padded seats on chairs dotted around round tables. Of course, the steward won't let me take a proper look. Finally, another flight of stairs, this time with paintings decorating it and a brass railing – obviously for the fanciest folk – and we must be on deck. We are still inside, but the air is fresh with the sea and I can hear it up here. This corridor only has doors on one side, and the panels have wallpaper in the middle of them. On the other side are a row of portholes. I stare out at the sea and sky.

I really am crossing the ocean. I saw it down below in the hold, just that glimpse, but I don't think I really believed it until I got up here.

We stop at a grand-looking wood-panelled door and the steward waves me aside while he gives three smart knocks. A long pause.

'Come,' says a booming voice. I swallow, wishing Rigel was back by my side as we enter the captain's office.

'Captain, sir.' The steward salutes. I try to copy him, thinking it must be the done thing, jerking my flattened hand to my forehead. It wins me another sharp tut.

'Mr Greeve-Birtwistle,' says the captain, 'who have we here?'

The captain looks me up and down with a frown. He has a solid rectangular face, his ears stick out a little and bright blue eyes glint from under the peak of his pearly-white cap. He reminds me a little of my second-eldest brother, Gerald, who always has his head in a book and only ever gives half a smile.

'Captain, this child was found *stowaway* in the hold,' says the steward, 'says she's cousin of Mr Cottam which seems like a likely tale. She's already broken into one of the trunks...'

'Has she now? Fetch Mr Cottam please, Mr Greeve-Birtwistle, I'll take it from here.'

With the steward gone, the captain sits at his desk, and I stand in front of it. He laces his fingers.

'I am Captain Rostron, and to whom am I speaking?' he says.

'Clara Scott, sir, I mean Captain, I mean Captain Rostron, sir,' I say, fumbling for words in a way that isn't like me at all. The way the captain is so dapper and calm is making me realize how scruffy I must look. What would Ma say with me in front of a ship's captain with sticky hands and goodness knows what?

'Just Captain is fine, Miss Scott,' says Captain

Rostron. 'Now we'll wait until Mr Cottam arrives.'

A knock at the door, right on cue.

I turn as Harry walks into the room. I'm so mightily glad to see him, I find myself swallowing back tears.

'Clara?' he says. 'What on earth ... how ...?'

The captain clears his throat. 'Mr Cottam, can you confirm that Miss Scott is your cousin as she claims?'

'Erm, yes, Captain, this is Clara Scott, all right. But I had no idea she was on board. Clara! How did you ...' The colour drains from his face and his jaw clenches. 'I swear it, Captain, I knew nothing about this.'

The captain says nothing and it dawns on me that he might think – they all might think – that Harry sneaked me on board for free.

My face grows hot.

'Let's allow the young lady to speak for herself,' says the captain. I gulp, deciding I have no option but the truth.

Once I've got past the embarrassing part of me hiding in the trunk in a tantrum, I admit I start to warm to my story, particularly when I describe the swing across the river in the crate. I even take the hoof pick out of my skirt pocket to demonstrate how I gouged my way out of the trunk and threw the maple syrup bottle for Rigel before realizing he wasn't a bear after all.

By the end of my fantastical tale I am quite breathless and sure I catch a twitch of a smile from Captain

Rostron, but Harry looks paler than ever and rubs his forehead.

'What were you thinking, Clara? You could have been seriously hurt, suffocated even! Please allow me to sincerely apologize on behalf of my cousin and her parents, Captain,' says Harry. 'Clara is known for her . . . high spirits and childish antics. Please dock my wages to pay for her passage.'

My cheeks burn. Childish antics? I'd have a smart retort ready if Frank had said that, but coming from Harry it cuts deep.

'It doesn't look like you had any choice in this matter, Mr Cottam,' said the captain, 'so that won't be necessary.'

'Harry didn't know a thing about it, no one did, it's not his fault—' I say.

The captain silences me with a raised hand, addressing Harry. 'Please return to your post and telegraph Miss Scott's family, as a matter of urgency. I will arrange a cabin and suitable chaperone for your cousin, so inform her parents she will be under my protection.'

'That is much appreciated, Captain, sir.' Harry salutes and turns sharply. He doesn't even look at me as he leaves the room.

My mouth drops open. No sign of fun cousin Harry now. My favourite cousin is going to be angry with me for ever.

All of this is completely unfair. I bite at my lips which are sore and dry.

If I hadn't been asked to fetch that heifer in the first place none of this would have happened.

Papa's fault, Frank's fault, Sarah's fault . . . If I hadn't slept in . . .

The captain runs his finger down a list on his desk, then clicks his tongue with a nod. He writes something on a sheet of crisp paper. When Mr Greeve-Birtwistle comes back I notice a strange bulge along the front side of his uniform jacket.

The shape of a ladle.

When he sees me looking, the steward's lip curls ever so slightly. If he's done something to Rigel . . . I'll . . .

I take a deep breath. I can't cause any more trouble for Harry's sake. But the captain should know a good dog is being kept down there in the dark.

'Please deliver this to Mrs Palmer in cabin 105 and return with her answer,' says Captain Rostron, handing Greeve-Birtwistle a note.

'That's first class, surely we can't expect—' The words explode from the steward with a spray of spittle, before he splutters, stopping himself. Eyes flashing, he continues in a calmer voice. 'Apologies, Captain, I mean to say there are bunks free in women's quarters third class that might be more . . . suitable.'

'I am aware of which berths are free and which are not, Greeve-Birtwistle, this is my ship. Despite . . . appearances, Miss Scott is Mr Cottam's cousin, from a respectable family and will require a suitable chaperone. You are dismissed.'

I can barely hold back my smile; it is so good to see the steward taken down a peg or two. I just hope he doesn't take his annoyance at me out on Rigel.

But my smile is no longer matched by Captain Rostron's. His face is stony.

'Miss Scott. You have caused significant embarrassment and upset for Mr Cottam, a valued member of my crew. I expect your behaviour from now on to be impeccable. There is a code of conduct at sea. No room for high jinks, wilful behaviour or any manner of . . . antics. Do I make myself clear?'

I bow my head. 'Yes, Captain,' I say, I'm sure this is a time for silence, but I can't very well leave Rigel as he is, can I?

'You may wait in the—'

'—Sorry, Captain, the dog being kept in the hold, Rigel, is alone in the dark, and it's not right to keep an animal like that. He saved my life, helped to get me out of the trunk, I would have thirsted to death.'

'Ah yes. I've had a complaint from a passenger. The animal ran amok in the ship's barbers, I hear.'

'Yes . . . but only because he'd been all cooped up! He's a really good, clever dog, I promise you that. Surely his owner could take him out a bit more, then he wouldn't—'

'Impossible,' says the captain.

'Then at least let me visit him, and his food and time outside need to be increased—'

'Miss Scott, I am the captain of a transatlantic liner. Being stowaway is a serious offence. I could have you forcibly removed from this ship at port and taken into police custody. You are in no position to make demands.'

His fierce low voice makes me tremble. I nod, looking down at my boots, dismayed when my tears start so quickly one drips off the end of my nose and splats on the captain's fine carpet.

'Yes, Captain. Sorry, Captain,' I mutter as I curtsey and turn, not daring to look at him again.

As I open the door his voice is soft. 'Miss Scott, you may rest assured the animal in the hold will be properly attended to.'

I risk a glimpse back behind me, but Captain Rostron is already paging through some papers.

7. 10 P.M. 12TH APRIL
FROM: TOURAINE
TO: TITANIC

DENSE FOG THIS NIGHT. CROSSED THICK
ICE FIELD.

UNITED STATES SENATE INQUIRY

Day 9 - 27th April 1912

Testimony of Sidney Daniels

SENATOR BOURNE: So on the 10th, 11th and 12th of April, what was the . . . mood among the third-class passengers? Any incidents of note?

- The mood was good, sir. I can only speak for the male passengers as that was my section. They spent their days in the general room, playing cards in the smoke room or up on third-class deck, and then all was quiet in the cabins. They'd come down sometimes, but they cleared out of the way while we wiped and mopped the rooms.

SENATOR BOURNE: Did any of the third-class passengers try to enter the second- and first-class areas?

- Not that I know of, sir. Oh I do remember they complained a little of the cold. The weather had become surprisingly sharp, you see, with freezing fog in the mornings, but we gave them extra blankets and all was well.

SENATOR BOURNE: Were you expecting there to

be a lifeboat drill? Did you hear of one being scheduled?

- I did. There was supposed to be a drill on Sunday the 14th. We were told that when we came on board.

SENATOR BOURNE: What about earlier, in Southampton? Were the lifeboats tested at all before you set sail?

- Not that I heard of. But I can't say if something different happened with the sailors. They were on board first.

SENATOR BOURNE: What was your impression of the lifeboats before the 14th of April? The number, the way they looked, anything at all.

- To be honest with you, sir, we were setting sail on a brand-new ship. I didn't give the lifeboats a second look, let alone count how many there were. Seems a rum thing to say now . . . but lifeboats were the last thing on anyone's mind.

My shoulders sag as I am led back along the ship's corridor by a young woman in a crisp apron.

'Hurry it along now, Miss Scott, I'm Susan, one of the first-class maids. I'll be taking you up to Mrs and Miss Palmer shortly, they're to be your chaperones. But I'll have to see to you first.' Blonde curls escape her mop cap, sticking to the edges of her rosy face.

She glances back down the corridor as if to check no one is behind us, then lowers her voice, eyes twinkling. 'You've got Greeve-Birtwistle in a right tizz – he's been blabbering all over the ship about your capers.'

Crowing about my adventure is the last thing I feel like doing, with Harry so disappointed in me and no idea if Rigel is back in the dark hold, but her friendly tone gives me a little hope that maybe I won't be hated by *everyone* on this ship. She leads me back down the stairs and along the corridors into what might be a crew area – the place is a maze – ending in a modest bathroom. Within minutes Susan has me stripped to my shift and into a lukewarm tub. After answering a barrage of questions, while being scrubbed and my hair washed and de-tangled, I stand in front of a narrow mirror wearing a shapeless grey pinafore and a too-big blouse bunching underneath it.

'It doesn't fit,' I say. I hate when I have to wear things that are too big for me. It always happens being the youngest and smaller than my sisters were at my age. 'It's all right really, I'll just wear—'

'Don't be a ninny,' she says, holding up my discarded dress. I hadn't noticed how bad it was. My dress is stained with water and dusted with wood clippings and crumbs. Even worse, tufts of black fur are stuck to it where I must have wiped my sticky syrupy fingers. In other circumstances I would have laughed at the sight. But what must Harold have thought, his stowaway cousin brought before the captain in such a state?

'You can't wear this up in first,' says Susan, then more

kindly, 'but it's good fabric. I'll see what I can do with it at the end of my shift.'

She's being decent, so I don't even complain when she rakes my hair into two tight plaits until my scalp tingles.

'Thank you, Susan,' I say.

She grins and drops her voice. 'I should be thanking you really – you're taking the Palmers' maid's room and giving me a break. Be a bit of a giggle for me to bunk with the other girls rather than making hot milk for Mrs Palmer at all hours.'

I try to smile, but from the way she talks I guess this isn't going to be much of a giggle for me.

Susan leads me so swiftly back along the corridors, I've no chance to get my bearings, but I sense the first-class corridor with its white-painted walls and elegant lighting is somewhere behind the captain's office. Susan knocks on the door and prods me in the back. I'm suddenly glad I've had a proper bath.

A young woman opens the door. Her sleeves are covered in white linen protectors like a baker or doctor. She towers over me. 'Clara Scott?' she says, narrowing shrewd hazel eyes that are rather deep-set beneath sturdy eyebrows. '*You* are Clara Scott?'

She looks so disgusted; I step back into Susan who gives me another jab.

'Oh no. This won't do at all,' continues the young

woman, who must be Miss Palmer. 'She's barely out of short skirts, Mother!'

True that I was in short skirts until a year or so ago, but that's only because it's more practical at the ranch.

'I am twelve years old,' I say, more indignantly than I mean to.

'And impertinent with it,' says Miss Palmer, folding her arms. 'I am not a nanny and nor do I wish to be, so this arrangement is utterly unsuitable. Susan, please take her back – to the captain, and tell him—'

An imperious voice interrupts. 'You'll do no such thing, close the door after you, Susan.'

Miss Palmer strides over to a desk where a brown camera box sits. 'Well, don't expect me to—'

'You *will* be Miss Scott's chaperone, Bernice, and you will be gracious about it. It's the least we can do for the captain, with you poking that camera around every corner of his ship.' The voice comes from an older lady sitting in a brocade armchair by a porthole in the spacious cabin; she looks up from her cross-stitch and over her glasses at me.

Miss Palmer folds her arms and leans back in her chair. 'And you think this will be good for your precious reputation, Mother, taking in a grotty little farm girl, a stowaway and thief to boot?'

I gasp again. 'The Scott family own a very respectable ranch—'

Mrs Palmer sighs and pats at the elaborate grey waves at the side of her head. With her heavy pearl jewellery and lace outfit she could not look more different than her plainly dressed daughter.

'Please don't be dramatic, Bernie. Not in the afternoon. I can't abide it.'

Bernice Palmer huffs and looks down at her work.

'Come closer, child, let me take a look at you.'

I step forward.

'I apologize for my daughter's manners, Miss Scott. I hope yours are more polished?'

'As if!' says Bernice. 'The last thing a photographer needs is to be associated with a scandal, how can I capture candid shots now? With her in tow and the whole ship gawking?'

'You know very well that crass language will give me a headache, Bernice!'

I raise my chin. What a cheek. It's pretty obvious this young woman is barely more than a girl herself. She reminds me of my eldest sister when the farrier's son took a girl from out of town to the harvest dance.

'I will do my best not to get in your way,' I say stiffly.

The elder woman stands, and pats my arm. 'Now, I've ordered tea and pastries and then Bernie and I shall spend some time in the saloon while you rest. You're exhausted, quite beside yourself, I can tell.'

My heart plunges like a ship's anchor. I'm dying to see where I am, get a sense of the *Carpathia*.

'I would very much like to get some fresh air, a walk on the decks . . .' I say, making my voice as quiet and humble as I can.

'Oh, it's quite cold, dear. Really very bitter. You're in my care now and will rest here for today,' says Mrs Palmer. 'Susan has moved out so you will use the maid's quarters.' She points to a door in the panelling.

I curl up on the narrow bed, and the last thought I have is there is no way in the world I will be able to sleep, before I sink into dreams of a darkness that smells of maple syrup, and a friendly black bear with ginger whiskers.

I wake to the hubbub of Mrs Palmer and Bernie dressing for dinner, Susan fussing around them. Before I can complain, the maid has manhandled me into one of Bernie's dresses – a puffy pale pink that doesn't suit me at all – and pins it so it almost fits. My hair is tugged by Mrs Palmer's spiky hog-hair brush, then teased into looping curls by my ears.

'There, Miss Scott, you really do look quite the lady,' says Susan.

I'm not so sure. When I look in the mirror, I see Bernie behind me, eyebrows raised, pinching her lips together. Susan fastens a short silk cape around my shoulders and I pull on the pair of gloves she hands me.

I've never dressed this fancy in my life, not even for Christmas.

The first-class dining room is something else. Rows of square tables covered in heavy damask cloths with snow-white folded napkins that look like twisted cones. A lamp on each table gives off a warm amber glow. More glass light fittings overhead twinkle off crystal glasses and silver cutlery. All the women are dressed like the Palmers – like me – the men in tail suits like they're at a wedding. I try not to look too dazzled.

Every face turns to stare and I realize my stowaway story has been gossip. The meal is painfully slow and at first I wonder how anyone can stand it. It soon dawns on me that this isn't a meal like I think of a meal, fighting with my brothers over the last heel of bread, everyone talking at once, then all finished, table cleared, done and dusted.

On a transatlantic liner, meals are an event. The main event. Sitting, eating, admiring each other's finest clothes and talking is what these steamer passengers do for *fun*. And I'm the latest subject of their chatter.

'How did you breathe inside the trunk?'

'Why did you climb into the luggage, child?'

'Weren't you terribly afraid?'

'My nerves would be shot to shreds!'

'Will your people be paying your fare?'

Every question brings me back to Harold's face when he saw me in the captain's cabin. That disappointment. And every mouthful of tender beef, warm bread and butter – even the towering meringue which would make my sisters squeal – just brings me back to Rigel licking syrup off my hand. The dog will have been taken off friendly Mr Chan the barber and sent back to the hold. Mr Greeve-Birtwistle and his ladle will have made sure of it.

This trip on RMS *Carpathia*, this experience living like I'm all hoity-toity could be the biggest adventure of my life and I can't enjoy one bit of it with that big, soft dog in the hold.

Could there be anything less fair? If so, I can't think of it.

At one point between them interrogating me and their other yawn-worthy conversation, an important-looking member of the crew, dressed in a plain suit rather than the dining steward's apron, passes a note to one of the men at our table. I had been introduced to him when we sat down and now I rake around in my mind for a name. Marshall, I think. His daughter had smiled at me.

'For you, Josephine,' says Mr Marshall.

Mrs Marshall takes the note and I see it is a marconigram, so it has come from Harry. My throat clenches. I long to see him, to explain properly what happened. The lady lays the slip of paper on the table and I read Harold's writing upside down.

```
FROM: TITANIC
TO: CARPATHIA. MARSHALL.

MESSAGE RECEIVED
LOVE LOTTIE.
```

'It's from *Titanic*,' says Mrs Marshall. 'My nieces are aboard; they attended a funeral in Paris and set sail a day before us, so they are now on their way back to New York.'

'Doesn't tell us a lot, does it?'

'Well, telegrams are expensive,' says Mrs Marshall, 'and the sole operator is kept extremely busy by all accounts. He's your cousin on your mother's side isn't he, Clara?'

I nod, relieved one of the younger men speaks before I have a chance to reply.

'I've been reading about *Titanic*, it is the queen of luxury liners! It's three hundred and fifty feet longer than *Carpathia*, and way more in tonnage. We intend to transfer to it for our return from our honeymoon, don't we, darling?'

His wife nods, the ringlets each side of her face bobbing. As she lowers her voice her eyes widen. 'We heard *Titanic*'s second-class cabins are as comfortable as first. You know it can carry three and a half thousand passengers and crew!'

'A floating palace, indeed,' says the man, 'it has Turkish baths, a squash court, a swimming pool . . . I ask you?'

I wonder where this *Titanic* liner is now. When I imagine it powering towards us, it gives me a strange feeling. Do ships ever collide? I will ask Harold when he's stopped being angry, if that day ever comes.

A very elderly lady draped in pearls purses her lips. '*Titanic* – pfft. It's the maiden voyage. No matter how ostentatious, you will never catch me travelling on an untried ship.'

The rest of the table roll their eyes but the young husband pats her hand with a smile. 'I read the *Titanic* designers declared it unsinkable.'

The woman gives a refined little snort.

RMS CARPATHIA

DINNER

CAVAIRE ŒUFS

CONSOMME CHATELAINE   TOMATO MEZZANI

SALMON STEAKS INDIENNE

HALIBUT HOLLANDAISE

BOUCHEES CREVETTES   PIED DE VEAU SUPREME

SIRLOIN AND RIBS OF BEEF

PHILADELPHIA CAPON

LEG OF MUTTON—CAPERS

EGG PLANT   BOILED RICE   VEGETABLE MARROW

BOILED AND BIGNON POTATOES

SPRING CHICKEN   FILET DE BŒUF

OMELETTES (TO ORDER)

APPLE PUDDING

PEACH TART   GELEE MADEIRE   COCONUT SANDWICH

ICE CREAM

DESSERT   COFFEE   TEA

Saturday
13th
April
1912

I roll over in bed yet again. The mattress is firmer than my bed at home which has been passed through a number of brothers and sisters. These sheets are thick and stiff, the blankets heavy. I know I should be grateful – I wouldn't want to spend another night in the hold, or a single moment more locked in that trunk, but my mind won't stop spinning, making me even more cross with myself for not sleeping.

Tomorrow I need to make things right with Harry and find a way to see to Rigel; it won't help if I'm yawning my head half off.

Mrs Palmer and Bernie have been snoring for some time. I wonder if Ma and Pa have got the message that I'm safe. When I imagine them searching the house for me while I was in the trunk it now seems a small, selfish trick to play. But when I picture them reading Harold's marconigram aloud at the dinner table and the gasps of my brothers and sisters I can't resist a little smile. Frank's face! They'll be jealous, I know they will. I sigh. Well, only because they don't know what it is really like. With cranky Miss Palmer keeping me permanently by her side, I'm likely to have as much fun as I had trapped in the hold.

Oh, poor Rigel.

Suddenly I can feel his huge shaggy head under my hand. I can't imagine it's going to be very easy to give Miss Palmer the slip tomorrow. This might be the only time I can get away.

I wriggle out of the covers and nudge open the door to the little cell of a room. On the shelf above a richly painted panel the black clock's hands slice its pearly face. Two in the morning.

Mrs Palmer snores softly, her teeth in a glass beside her bed, head propped high on her pillows. Miss Palmer is completely hidden under her covers, aside from a single dark braid of hair, snaking across the sheets.

If I'm caught wandering at night, I will cause even

more embarrassment for Harold than I already am.

Although, is that actually possible?

I swing my legs out of bed.

The trick is not to get caught.

I force myself to tread slow and light along the dimly lit corridor in my borrowed boots. I didn't ask permission but my chaperone seems mighty keen to get me all trussed up in her daughter's clothes, so I'm just doing as I'm told . . . really. The boots aren't a bad fit over the woollen bed socks Mrs Palmer made me wear. I also took Miss Palmer's long wool overcoat, pleased to find a beret and gloves tucked in the pocket. I need them right away; Mrs Palmer was right about the cold.

I've always been quite proud of how I find my way back on the farm – even in the forest I know which track to take without thinking about it – but the ship is like a rabbit warren. The fact I've never seen the outside of it makes it even trickier. But the Palmers haven't woken, the ship is almost weirdly silent and I am looking forward to seeing Rigel. I remember at least three flights of a staircase near the rear of the boat.

I get lucky when I find a map of RMS *Carpathia* on the back of a door closing a flight of stairs down to third-class. I grin, tracing where I am now and find the hold, then I race along a wide corridor that cuts through the lower central part of the ship like its backbone.

There are three holds here but I needn't worry which door at the end of the dimly lit corridor will lead to Rigel. As soon as I try the handle I hear his familiar growl. I only smile for a second before the dog breaks out into his gruff bark.

The door to the hold is locked. Of course it is – Greeve-Birtwistle wasn't going to make that mistake twice.

I crouch at the keyhole and whisper into the brass lock. 'Rigel, it's me, quiet now.'

Rigel stops growling but continues barking and I hear the clatters of his claws on the stairs the other side of the door, then a gust of breath warms my face.

'Shhh, please boy.'

He doesn't shhh, he barks harder. I can't blame him, locked down here in the guts of the ship. I didn't shush either.

Horsefeathers! I can't leave Rigel now, it seems too cruel, crueller somehow than never coming here at all, but I need to run, now, because this barking will surely wake up the—

'Miss Scott again?' says a familiar voice.

I almost jump out of my skin and spin around. Mr Chan, the barber. Thank goodness! He is dressed in a long, rather dapper fawn cashmere coat and a yellow scarf, and his dark eyes glint from beneath a trapper hat with fur flaps. What is he doing here? But I'm glad. I allow myself to breathe out.

'Miss Scott. You've sure put a bee in Greeve-Bristlewizz's bonnet,' he says with a chuckle.

'What are you doing here, Mr Chan?'

'After your dog's first haircut he's taken a bit of a shine to me and I'm the only one who could get him down here. I offered to see to his night walk on deck. Greeve-Busterwind didn't have much choice since the beast hates his guts.'

'I'm glad. He threatened Rigel with a ladle,' I say, my cheeks heating with anger at the thought.

'No surprise there, he'd like to threaten most people with a ladle. Isn't like me to offer charity work, I require eight hours' sleep at the very least and can't stand the cold. But there's something about this oversized pooch got me going soft.' He draws out a large key. 'You've woken the beast now, so move yourself.'

When Mr Chan swings open the door, Rigel bounds straight past him and licks at my hand. I'd forgotten how big and fluffy he is, a big black mop of a hound. I ruffle under his ears.

'Why is he down in the hold and not with his owner?' I say.

'Ah – well I did a little investigating. He was a fisherman's dog up in Nova Scotia. When the old fella died he was left to his nephew, a hotelier in Naples. He's in the cargo hold because he actually is . . . cargo. Poor beast.'

I frown. You can't treat a dog like he's a piece of furniture, like Gramma's things in the trunk. Rigel sits by my feet and I rest my hand on his head. He looks up at me, eyes shining and I feel that bright warm feeling in my heart, like I get with Folly.

'Why don't I take him up on deck for a turn?' I say. 'I'm dressed warm enough. Look – he'll be calmer with me.'

'Best not, said I'd do it as a favour to Captain Rostron and he's the one person on this ship I have a lot of respect for.' Mr Chan fastens a rope around Rigel's collar. 'Come on, buddy.'

I have an idea. I click my fingers quietly, too quiet for the man to hear. But dogs have super hearing.

Rigel's ears shift, his black eyes on mine. I mouth 'sit'.

'Get moving, hound,' says the man. He produces a piece of ham wrapped in a napkin. 'This will shift him.' The huge dog looks up at him with sad eyes and his wet nose trembles at the salty smell of the ham, but still he sits.

I raise a hand palm up behind Chan's back and mouth 'stay'.

No growling.

No barking.

Definitely no moving.

Rigel really is a good dog.

Mr Chan spins around without warning and I don't drop my hand in time.

'Ohhh, you are a one.'

I shrug innocently. 'Perhaps it will be easier if I'm not here.' I turn to walk away and Rigel releases one hard low bark.

The barber rubs his face.

'Mr Chan,' I whisper, 'what if you never saw me? What if I stole your keys and released Rigel, walked him on deck and returned him and nobody including yourself was any the wiser?'

The barber shakes his head but hands me the rope. 'You're too smart for me, little lady, especially at this hour,' he yawns.

'I can hardly be in more trouble than I already am, and the poor dog does need to get some air.'

I've wheedled my own way enough times to know when I've won. Mr Chan frowns at my grin.

'Don't get too cocky, Greeve-Birtwistle will have told his son all about you.'

'His son?' I say, confused at what the steward's family has got to do with anything.

'Third Officer Greeve. We've got one Greeve swinging his weight around below deck and the other doing the same up above. Lucky us.'

18

Rigel lumbers up the stairs without a single pull on the rope, blending into the shadows left by the solitary lamp high on the wall. I feel a strange bolt of pride or joy, or something between the two, to see how he doesn't pull at the leash and glances back at me. This dog likes me. Respects me even. Just like Folly. Animals don't pretend and they don't accept excuses if you treat them badly.

It gets colder the higher I go, and also quieter as I suppose I'm getting further from the engine. At the first-class cabin corridor I take a left instead of right to the

Palmers' cabin, and finally reach the door that leads out on to deck. The icy air needles my face and I stop to button the overcoat right to the neck and pull the beret down over my ears. Rigel bashes me with his plumy tail and bounces on his front paws like a pup.

After 2 a.m. the deck is as empty as I'd hoped. I lead Rigel up and down the first-class promenade, grabbing a steamer rug to wrap around my shoulders so I'm almost completely bundled. Rigel leads me from side to side as he sniffs at everything. We walk past the giant red funnel with its black painted top. It's magnificent, I've never seen anything like it, and this isn't even a big steamer. I remember what the passengers were saying about *Titanic* – the biggest liner to ever set sail. I was sure someone said it had four of these funnels. Four!

I walk towards the back of the ship, passing four lifeboats, taking it all in. The promenade becomes narrower. The air nips my bare ankles and I shiver. At the stern – I don't know much about boats but I think this is the right name for the back – I cross over the width of the ship, again marvelling at the sheer size of it, and start to walk up the other side. A sliver of moon glitters and I'm now facing the direction the steamship is travelling, the stronger wind forcing freezing water from the corners of my eyes. When I stop in the lee of the large cabin that sits on deck, the funnel rising up from the middle of it, Rigel wags impatiently so his whole bottom end wiggles. I pull the belt of the coat tighter, crossing the steamer rug across my chest and tucking the ends into the belt.

'All right, Rigel,' I say, burrowing my hands deep into Rigel's warm neck fur, 'not everyone wears a permanent fur coat like you.'

I'm determined to explore the whole boat, right to the – what was it called? – bow. I walk more briskly beneath the funnel and back towards the front mast. Rigel stops, ears lifting.

'Not here, Rigel,' I say, looking nervously at the row of black portholes behind me. Does anyone sleep up here?

But Rigel drags me to the railing, nose in the air, sniffing. He growls, but his tail wags gently.

'Rigel, come.' I try again to pull him.

'What have you seen?' I whisper, bending to follow Rigel's eyeline out across the sea. Imagine seeing a dolphin. What would Frank say about that! The dog treats me to a quick lick on the cheek then releases a small ruff of a bark. Now his tail is upright, back straight, fluff standing up. He's raising his hackles. Another louder bark. He won't be dragged. Can Rigel see or sense something out there?

I scan over the sea. What on earth – I try to think of a visit to the New York Aquarium we took when I was younger. There could be fish, seals, dolphins, whales . . . maybe an octopus or a shark?

But I can't see a thing. The moon is too skinny to give enough light.

Rigel's gentle woofs turn abruptly into a barrage of barking and he springs up to rest his feet on the first railing. I grab his collar, his huge shaggy head coming up as tall as me.

'Careful, boy,' I say, tucking my arm around his middle as I stare out and catch sight of something breaking the surface.

I don't even hear Rigel's barking any more, I'm too busy trying to make sense of what I'm seeing.

It is smooth, curved. Gleaming in the faint moonlight. Wait, there's more than one, in a row, one behind the other, three, now four, and moving as fast as the boat. What are they?

They sink below the surface and rise again. At the same time. At exactly the same time, and I see it's not a group of sea creatures.

It's one. One huge animal. Each gleaming curve is a loop of something very long. And to keep up with the ship – very fast.

I grip Rigel more tightly, his barks shaking my whole body as I scan for another glimpse.

What in heavens is it? So big, impossibly so – at least

it looked that way. A whale? No wonder Rigel . . .

There it is again! It's turning, it's coming towards the ship, and at high speed. I gasp. Can it hear us?

'Shhh Rigel,' I hiss in the barking dog's ear.

'What is the meaning of this racket?'

I whirl around to see Captain Rostron, in a long overcoat and nightcap.

13TH APRIL
FROM: CORSICAN
TO: VIRGINIAN

PASSED HEAVY FIELD ICE AND NUMEROUS
BERGS

19

Even in his nightcap Captain Rostron looks impressive.

Rigel chooses that moment to blast off another volley of deep urgent barks out to sea, but the creature that was definitely heading directly towards us – wasn't it? – has gone.

The captain is here. Where I am definitely *not* supposed to be.

I try to grab Rigel's chops between my hands and make him look at me and stop his racket, but he won't stop staring out at the place the sea creature just was.

'Enough, Rigel, there's nothing there now!'

But there definitely had been something there. Something vast and . . . lengthy. Not the same shape as a whale. Long like the eels I've sometimes seen in a tub of water at market, writhing in slick knots.

A colossal eel? I shudder.

The captain joins me and Rigel at the railing, the dog still growling and barking in a sort of rhythm. But Captain Rostron doesn't attempt to quiet him.

'All right, boy, what do you see?' he says quietly, laying a hand on the dog's back.

I blink up at him. Should I tell him what Rigel is making all the fuss about? No – surely he wouldn't believe me.

I try to follow the dog's eyeline – and now the captain's gaze – across where the wake of the boat blends into the flat seas. Nothing.

No – something. That break of the surface again, thankfully further from the ship.

'There,' I yell, forgetting myself completely as I grab a fistful of the captain's sleeve, pointing, not daring to tear my eyes away as one bump surfaces, and then another behind it. Black, gleaming, slick. Huge.

'Where? I can't—'

I lean into the captain to point but the beast is too quick, and I rush out my words over Rigel's growls. 'It's gone, there were three, four parts of it out of the water, like curved hills – the trail . . . see.'

The churn of water continues as if the creature is only just below the surface.

'Yes,' hisses Captain Rostron, raising an eyeglass. 'I see the turbulence now – it is circling the prow. Come.'

I follow the captain.

It?

What?

Is he pulling my leg? Because I wasn't expecting him to act like this.

I can't spot anything else but Rigel confirms what the captain is saying, because I almost lose hold of the rope leash when he tugs me. I run around the cabins to the opposite deck. Rigel simply whines now as the captain and I lean on the rails, scanning the black expanse of sea. The night seems spookily silent without his barking.

'I think it's gone.'

The captain continues to scan the ocean, stopping at times to raise his eyeglass. Rigel sits and I move from foot to foot, realizing my toes are completely numb.

'Is it a giant . . . eel? Or a type of whale?'

'Neither, Miss Scott, nor anything so commonplace,' says the captain, turning to me. His eyes sparkle as if the moon itself is trapped inside them.

Captain Rostron bends slightly to hold Rigel's huge

head between his large slim hands. I brace myself for more barks or that deep growl but Rigel pants softly, tongue hanging out and tail wagging like a black flag. 'A sensitive animal . . . despite appearances.'

I smile and pat Rigel as he gazes from the captain to me, then back again. The dog sits next to me.

'It is you he trusts.'

I ruffle Rigel between the ears, mind back on what I've just seen. 'What was that thing, Captain Rostron?'

The captain stands straight. 'Would you and Rigel care to join me inside for a cup of chocolate?'

I glance down at Rigel, whose eyes are fixed on me, steady. I shiver at the thought of being in the warm. And the chocolate. Then I remember the way that thing beneath the waves was coming straight for me and Rigel and my shivering won't stop.

'Yes, Captain. Yes please.'

20

The officers' saloon is a small dark-wood-panelled room and cosier than I could have hoped. I loosen the steamer rug from around my shoulders, relieved when Rigel flops down at my feet, his body soon warming them so my toes tingle. The captain excuses himself and must have found the night porter or prepared them himself because he is soon back, carrying a tray with two steaming mugs. I take one, wrapping my icy hands around it in relief and only then notice the captain is now fully dressed in his uniform. He must see my surprise.

'I won't be sleeping again tonight, Miss Scott,' he says, and lays a leather folder on the table. He unclips a brass catch and removes a sheaf of papers. Then he waits, chin raised, as he peers down his nose, watching me.

I eye him back over the edge of my mug of chocolate and then look down at his papers. I can beat every member of my family in a staring contest, but might have met my match in this captain.

'If you become too weary at any point you must let me know.'

Rigel is peacefully warming not just my feet but halfway up my legs with his huge body. The chocolate is rich and creamy.

'I'm quite all right now, sir,' I say.

'Would I be right in thinking Mrs and Miss Palmer might not want to share a cabin with our observant canine friend?'

'I'll say.' I cover my mouth, not meaning to sound rude, but it just slipped out when I imagined Miss Palmer's face.

'I thought as much so have asked the night porter to prepare one of the first-class cabins for you both. It was closed for refurbishment but should be comfortable enough.'

Both? I slurp my chocolate as I break into a grin.

'For me and Rigel to stay together?'

The captain nods, and his lips twitch only slightly, the curved lines around his mouth deepening.

'Rigel. An unusual name. Rigel is a star in the constellation of Orion, no less, and one of the brightest in the sky. An original navigational star used by ancient navigators.'

I grin and ruffle Rigel's head. His strange name has a rather grand meaning. Whoever named him really thought about it.

'Fitting for a sea dog, I would say,' says Captain Rostron, then makes a steeple with his hands.

'My stewards are constantly complaining about the barking. I would be grateful if you could be a . . . steadying influence on this bright and rather noisy star.'

This time I splutter into my chocolate, and have to wipe up some droplets with the sleeve of my coat at the thought of what my sisters would say hearing me, Clara Scott, being described by this ocean liner captain as a 'steadying influence'. I almost ask if I can have that in writing, but the captain looks quite severe once again.

'The Palmers are still your official chaperones, Miss Scott. I will require they know where you are and you will attend meals with them at least some of the time, depending on how Rigel settles.'

'Yes – yes, I'd love to keep Rigel with me if I can, we're . . .' I trail off, not sure how to describe it.

'. . . on rather cordial terms?'

'Yes. Friendly,' I say, and narrow my eyes, suddenly feeling like I've missed something important. Why is Rigel suddenly getting this special treatment when the captain allowed him to be locked in the hold until now?

But it is happening, and I'm so pleased that I don't have to leave him alone in the dark again that I start to babble. 'I guess he must have been valued by his former owner.'

'The fishing dogs of Newfoundland are quite renowned. Powerful swimmers with a loyal and gentle temperament. And it seems he's used to affection so was likely a companion.'

I ruffle Rigel's head, remembering Mr Chan said he was given away in a will . . . like a carriage clock. It's not fair.

'That's agreed then,' said the captain, hand on his papers. 'Now. There is some information I would like to share with you, Miss Scott. But before I do, could you please describe to me again exactly what you saw out at sea. Before I arrived this evening, and when I was by your side.'

I do as he asks, his probing questions making me remember things I hadn't realized I'd seen, like there being a ridge of some kind along the back of the beast. He takes notes and even makes me draw a small picture to accompany what he has written.

Finally he turns back to his papers. 'You see, Miss Scott, this is a subject of special interest for me.'

He has my full attention. I'd like very much to know what 'this' is.

'Sea serpents have been lore of the sea for centuries. There was a famous encounter by HMS *Daedalus* in 1848. The creature seen was "enormous", some sixty foot long, with "something like seaweed washed about its back". Captain McQuhae had drawings made immediately after it was seen, including this.' Captain Rostron pushes a sheet of paper across to me.

Sea serpent? Is that what the captain is really talking about? I'm not sure what to say. I didn't see the creature's head, but could it be the same thing?

Captain Rostron continues. 'Yarns about monsters of the deep are hardly a new thing, sailors have been reporting sightings since they first crossed the oceans. This is 1912, we are in an age of science, of reason – and superstitions generally have no useful place in the proper running of a ship. But so many men – good and reliable witnesses – have had experiences that cannot be dismissed.'

My heart drums in my chest. He is serious.

We had been right there, close to it on the deck. Could it have reared out of the water?

'There's something else,' I say, and he pins my face with his eyes and nods, hands interlinked over the drawing.

'Before you arrived it turned. It was coming straight towards me and Rigel,' I say.

The captain tilts his head, and jots something down. 'Thank you, Miss Scott. Thank you for telling me that. And . . . let's keep this conversation and our sighting between ourselves. For now.'

After Captain Rostron assures me the decks are too high for any creature to reach, even a mythical beast like a sea serpent, I am a little calmer. He walks me to the first-class cabin, at the far end of the corridor from the Palmers, and hands me the key.

'Please do try to get some sleep, Miss Scott,' he says, 'but contact me – and only me – if our furry friend here detects anything else. Seems Rigel here with his superior canine senses can act as an alarm. My cabin is just in front of the officers' saloon, so you're as close by as possible. Don't hesitate.'

That does make me feel a little better.

'I will. Thank you,' I say. I try to stifle a yawn as I open the door. The captain tips his white cap at me. I imagine Ma's face at the sight of the grand and dignified captain talking to me this way and grin.

My new cabin is a mirror image of the Palmers'. I quickly strip off Bernie's coat and kick off her boots and then wriggle down into the blankets of a huge soft bed like Mrs Palmer's. No need for me to sleep in the maid's room if I've got this all to myself.

I close my eyes. The ship barely rocks. My feet are cold again despite the puffy comforter. Rigel settles at the end of the bed on the floor with a sigh. That must have been where he slept with his old master. Then I sit up. 'Come, Rigel,' I whisper and pat the bed beside me.

Plenty of room for two. He's not a working dog or even a companion now. Rigel is my friend.

I wake the warmest I've been since on board, Rigel's heavy head across my feet, gently snoring. I lie for a few moments remembering what I saw, what the captain said about the sea serpent. I can't help shaking my head in disbelief. But if a man like Captain Rostron believes . . .

A knock at the door. I brace myself for Rigel's barks but he simply raises his shaggy head.

'Who is it?'

'Bernie Palmer, of course. Open up will you?'

I think guiltily about the older girl's coat and boots as I pad over to the cabin door in her nightgown. Rigel follows and I ruffle his head. Would she have woken worried, raised an alarm even? Just as things are settling down with Captain Rostron confiding in me, I can't get into more trouble; I need to see Harold today. But Bernie Palmer is holding my own clothes in a bundle, freshly laundered and pressed. I take the pile from her and see her brown box camera hanging around her neck.

'A very strange note was slid under our door this morning. Apparently our maid's room isn't good enough for the stowaway.' She looks almost cheerful this morning but I'm not sure if she's jesting. 'That lily-livered Susan seems to think your mutt will eat her so I had to come myself. Well, are you going to leave me standing in the corridor?'

I usher her in.

Rigel releases one sharp bark but Miss Palmer doesn't flinch. She maintains eye contact with me, while she reaches out a closed fist to the dog. To my surprise Rigel nudges her hand with his nose and gives it a very small lick.

'There. I won't bother you, you won't bother me, and we'll get along just fine,' she says to the dog. 'Well, get dressed quickly, Mother wants you at lunch.'

I spin around. It's after twelve – I've never slept in like this!

'Sorry. I took your coat and boots—'

'Never mind that – you keep them,' she says, with an impatient wave of her hand. 'Mother always overpacks for us, I have others. Word has spread, you know, that the captain has a special interest in you and this animal. And I'm wondering why that might be.'

I look into Miss Palmer's hooded hazel eyes beneath those fierce brows. She has both hands on her camera.

'I guess he likes dogs?' I say.

The captain said to keep quiet but I do glance at the camera, wondering if she could capture the creature we saw on film . . .

When I look up it feels like she's been reading my mind.

'If there's something strange happening on this ship, I will find out, Clara Scott,' she says. She drops on one knee in front of Rigel, looks down into her camera and I hear the click of the shutter. She winds the side.

'Hey!' I say, frowning.

'What?' she says.

'Well . . .' I'm suddenly not sure why I feel quite so irritated with her doing that.

'I have permission from Captain Rostron to take candid shots of life aboard RMS *Carpathia*. He says he has nothing to hide. Do you?'

I roll my eyes at her. That's not the point. She turns on her heel. 'See you at lunch, and don't think of bringing your bodyguard with you. Oh, and don't call me Miss Palmer either, reminds me of my mother. It's Bernie.'

22

I'm relieved to be able to rush through lunch with the excuse of getting back to Rigel.

Only trouble is, I'm now stuck with either Mrs or Miss Palmer. This afternoon it's Miss – Bernie. Now that he isn't locked in the hold or alerting us to a sea monster, Rigel is calm and even gathers smiles from a few of the passengers as we trail along behind Bernie, stopping every time she wants to photograph something, and getting colder and colder. Of course Rigel and I get stares as Bernie predicted. Everyone must know by now that I am the stowaway and they've probably all now heard about the escapade in the barber's salon.

I hear them whisper about Rigel 'rampaging', which is a bit of an exaggeration.

Turns out that Rigel is actually a rather patient dog. He doesn't mind stopping for the photographs and rests at my feet with his head on his paws if Bernie greets someone.

But then a few things happen at once. First Bernie spots a crowd forming further along the deck, peering out into the water. She rushes ahead of me, winding on the camera gripped in front of her and is so determined people move out of her way.

I stare out, stomach rising to my throat. Is it the sea serpent again? Should I be telling the crowd to get back, get away from the railings? But Rigel isn't barking . . .

Then I see. Three mounds, then four, no . . . six. Smooth grey skin on their curved fins.

'A pod of dolphins,' says the older man standing next to me. I watch as they dip and break the surface, flashing long noses and small lidded black eyes. They weave in and out of each other, keeping pace with the ocean liner, playing with the foam of its wake. Bernie snaps away on her camera and I now know for sure that this was not what I saw last night.

Everyone is looking at the dolphins. Oohing and aahing.

Then Rigel barks. Once, twice. His tail up straight. Telling me.

I tear my eyes from the dolphins and scan beyond them and the ripples they are making. More swells. A rise in the surface, then another ten feet away, waters part over skin darker than the dolphins, darker than the deep-teal sea.

'Shut your dog up,' says Bernie through gritted teeth.

I ignore her, tracking the sea serpent as it remains just below the surface. No one is looking, no one is seeing. Then a twisting spin of water and it turns to swim towards the smaller creatures. From the corner of my eye I see the dolphins leap out of the water in a smooth arc and there's a cascade of laughter and calls of joy at the sight. No one sees a head rise up.

Huge. Monstrously huge, like nothing I've seen. Long rounded snout, light eyes with a line through the middle. Tiny needle teeth, broken up with much bigger fangs that overhang the bottom jaw . . .

Rigel leaps, his front paws up on the railing.

I haul him back, terrified he'll jump in.

His claws slip on the smooth metal and nudge into Bernie.

Her camera falls to the floor.

Horsefeathers!

Bernie snatches up the camera. The crowd turn on

me and Rigel, who – after the disappearance of the sea monster – now wags calmly at my side. It must have truly gone.

'Your dog scared them away. That dolphin pod might have followed us all the way to Europe!' shouts one of the crowd.

'I've made five crossings and this is the first time we've seen them.'

'Mama, where have the dolphins gone?'

I'm pretty sure it wasn't Rigel that scared the dolphins away, but the giant sea serpent sneaking up on them. I hold my head up high as there's nothing I can say, but suddenly I'm surrounded by men, women and children, and all are glaring at me.

Rigel growls. Oh no, if he thinks I'm in danger I don't know what he'll—

'What's this? Clara?' a familiar voice cuts through the crowd.

'Harry?' I call out and then the crowd melts away as quickly as it formed and my cousin is looking down on me, frowning. Rigel makes a rumble in his throat, but when Harry offers the back of his hand he licks and wags. I breathe out.

'Making more new friends, cousin?' he says and his brow lifts. 'You have somehow made a good impression on the captain at least. Although you're making me rather more well known than I like to be.'

'Tell me about it,' I say. 'That's Rigel, not me.'

'Sounds like you are partners in crime,' he says. 'Now is my cousin going to take a walk with me or not, I've only got ten minutes to stretch my legs.'

Bernie is sitting on a bench inspecting her camera.

Please don't let it be broken.

But with Harry here and certainly not as upset as he was, I don't want Bernie to get in the way of me talking to him so I walk straight on.

'Now tell me about these dolphins. Rigel can sense them?' he says. 'I wonder if that's to do with vibration, that's how sound travels. Sound is simply many tiny movements travelling through a material.'

I don't know what he means but I nod, relieved to be side by side with Harry cheerful again like I've always known him to be. I describe the dolphins and how Rigel sensed them, but don't tell him about the sea serpent. I can't tell him Captain Rostron saw it too, so I can't tell it at all.

When we reach the stern of the ship Harry stops. 'Please do what the Palmers say, Clara, you're in safe hands there,' he says.

'Yes,' I say. I haven't exactly made a promise.

Harry doesn't offer to show me his Marconi room and I just about manage not to ask him. I'm desperate to see it, but know I can't be interfering with his work right now. I'm surprised at myself being patient for once.

After Harry disappears back to his post I find a new bounce in my step. I take a slow walk around the quieter parts of the ship with my head high, and that's where Bernie finds me again.

'You didn't apologize or at least check to see if the camera was in one piece after you whacked it out of my hands,' says Bernie, barely taking a breath before she continues, 'and now I've had to chase around the whole vessel looking for you. I told Mother this wouldn't work. You really are the most selfish child.'

She jabs her hands on her hips and taps her foot. I actually did feel sorry about the camera, but I don't feel like saying it now.

'Is your camera working?' I say instead, bracing myself for a less than friendly response.

'Actually it is, no thanks to you or to that hound.' Her voice becomes low and dangerously slow. 'Now, I've told Mother I fancy you are rather tired and she has agreed you should spend the rest of today in your room.'

I frown. I should find the captain, tell him what I saw. But I can't say that.

'Rigel needs exercise,' I say instead.

I narrow my eyes and she narrows hers.

'Then we shall take two turns of the deck with the

dog. And you'll lead the way.'

I'm not going to win this one.

For the rest of Saturday I am banished to my room with a copy of what sounds like the most boring book in the world, *Little Women*. Rigel snores on the bed and even my meals are brought to me, but by the time the sun sets I've actually begun to like Jo March and her sisters.

I have to give it to Bernie Palmer, she knows how to settle a score.

Sunday

14th

April

1912

5.35 P.M. 14TH APRIL
FROM: CARONIA
TO: TITANIC COMMANDER

ALL BEST WISHES SUCCESS MUCH LOVE
GEORGE AND KATIE RIGGS

23

The next day I watch out for the captain at lunch, but there is no sign of him and I suppose he mostly eats with the officers. Once again it is dead calm and cold, the sea like a glass lid covering a grey world below.

I'm allowed back out of the cabin, but only when I promise old Mrs Palmer I'll accompany her to 'take the air'. Turns out this means sitting still in the cold. At least as a first-class passenger I can use one of the fancy wooden steamer chairs. The deck steward gives me a long look and I imagine him reporting back to Mr

Greeve-Birtwistle, but for once I'm actually where I'm supposed to be so I stare back, bold. I wrap myself in a steamer blanket as Rigel gnaws a bone one of the galley hands brings up for him. When he's finished I throw it overboard and a couple of small children stare.

'Mother says we are not to throw anything overboard. Not one thing,' says the younger of the two, a very small girl who can't be more than four, clutching a dog-eared toy rabbit.

'She was only throwing the bone over, silly. That doesn't count as it's trash,' says the boy who is a good bit older, not anywhere near my age but almost as tall.

'Mother said not one thing,' insists the girl, frowning, but the glare is suddenly wiped off her face by a giggle.

'Hey – what are you—' she squeals as Rigel's huge head burrows into her coat pocket.

At first I think the older boy will tell her off, or snatch her away, but then he laughs too and they both ruffle around the dog's ears. Rigel does something I've not seen before; he collapses to the deck and rolls over on his back to show his middle. Both children tickle the dog's huge tummy.

'Oh, Rigel, you silly pup,' I say. He nuzzles the girl's coat pocket again.

'Your dog has a good nose,' says the boy. 'My sister Yolanda is always smuggling biscuits and cakes out of the dining room. I think she likes seeing if the stewards will stop her.'

'They never do,' giggles the little girl. Rigel is still lying on his back, now somehow with the girl's pink ribbon in his mouth. She tugs on the other end of it.

'You want to play, big doggy, want to play,' she sings. Rigel releases a gentle growl and rolls back and forth on the deck, tail wagging. I can't help but laugh.

The boy reaches out a hand for me to shake but before we can introduce ourselves a shrill voice interrupts.

'Yolanda! Come away at once, what have I told you about strange dogs? What are you thinking, John? I expect to know better.'

A lady herds the children away from Rigel, pushing them behind her back. My heart drops to see who else is there. Mr Greeve-Birtwistle, with a very smug look on his face.

'This animal was threatening my daughter,' the lady says, after directing the sorry-looking children to go back to their cabin.

'He was only playing,' I say, but she steps towards me wagging her finger.

'If I had my way, madam, this dog would be in the hold and, trust me, I have told the captain as such in no uncertain terms,' says Mr Greeve-Birtwistle.

'Well it's regrettable he hasn't listened to your

concerns,' says the lady. 'Not everybody thinks it's a terribly big lark to have a stowaway and a beastly dog in first class. I don't know what the captain or the Palmers are thinking. She's from a farming family I heard?'

I feel my cheeks flush at her rudeness, not only talking about me like that, but looking at Mr Greeve-Birtwistle and never once meeting my eyes.

'Now hold your horses,' I say, 'there's no need to go around insulting—'

Rigel growls and I grab his collar just in time as he takes a step towards her. She leaps back, which anyone knows is the worst thing to do with a dog because they love to chase. He growls again and I see the little girl's ribbon is hanging out from his mouth. Not exactly a good look between bared teeth.

'But, Mama, I—'

'Hush, Yolanda. Keep that beast away from my children,' she says, backing away, herding her children behind her.

The woman turns and I see a small crowd have gathered. Exactly what I've been trying to avoid.

'Mama!' says the little girl. 'My Babbit! He's drowning!'

And there in the water is the girl's toy, bobbing in the boat's wake. She must have thrown it in.

'Oh, for pity's sake, Yolanda,' says her mother. 'Well,

it's gone now, nothing can be done.'

The little girl's face creases then turns red, and she releases a heartbroken shriek. At the same time the rope yanks out of my hand, and with the skittering sound of claws against the metal rail Rigel bounds in a perfect arc, overboard.

'Rigel!' I scream as the black dog splashes into the water, and it seems a very long moment before he bobs to the surface and starts to swim in circles.

I catch my breath, remembering what the captain said. Rigel was a fisherman's dog way up north. His coat will be made for cold water. He wouldn't have jumped in unless he could do this – would he?

'Doggy's got Babbit!' says the little girl between hiccupping breaths. And she's right. In the dog's jaws is the sodden toy. But the liner is steaming ahead and even as Rigel paddles with those giant feet of his, he's already dropping behind.

'Help him!' I yell. I spin to Mr Greeve-Birtwistle, the last person I need but the nearest member of staff. 'You need to tell the captain, please, help him.'

Mr Greeve-Birtwistle acts like he hasn't heard me and tears start up in my eyes.

Rigel is getting further away but paddling so hard. Oh – I can't bear this.

'Help him, someone, please!' I yell and spin again to find old Mrs Palmer gripping a short man's arm, a man in a familiar deerstalker hat. Mr Chan! She is talking into his ear but before she's finished he darts off, running at top speed through the crowd towards the front of the boat. Now I can only just make out Rigel's black head against the white wake of the liner, and my voice is hoarse with yelling.

A bell rings and I can't believe it when the vibration of the ocean liner changes and the ship slows.

I blink back tears. Captain Rostron is stopping *Carpathia*? For Rigel? I hardly dare believe it.

'This will slow the crossing and I've got a meeting – outrageous, they can't about-turn for an ownerless dog.'

'We aren't turning, just slowing down. And look – the dog is catching up!'

The voice is right. Rigel gets closer and closer. But there's something else, something I am beginning to recognize now. The water swells in lumps one behind the other. A flash of that gleaming dark skin before the creature slips back below the surface.

'Rigel! Watch out, Rigel!' I scream.

'Someone explain to the child the giant mutt is getting closer now so there's no need for this to-do.'

They haven't seen it. But the creature is there, just beneath the surface, creating telltale swirls in the water if you know what to look for.

I remember its spiky snaggled teeth and scream again for Rigel.

The sea serpent draws circles, a moving ring around Rigel, but the dog calmly paddles as if he hasn't a care in the world. I remember how the dolphins disappeared at the sea serpent's arrival. Boneheaded dog!

But the loops don't get any smaller, the beast isn't enclosing my friend; instead they grow fainter until there is only a trail of bubbles.

Now Rigel has made it to the side of the ship. The sea serpent has gone.

One of the *Carpathia*'s lifeboats swings out on its winch with two sailors sat inside and is lowered down the side. Rigel seems to know exactly what to do and leaps aboard in one giant wet bound. He shakes himself off, soaking the two sailors. I push through the crowd to the winch as the boat is hauled back up the side of the ocean liner and Rigel bounds out.

'You big goof, I could have lost you for ever!' I grasp my friend tight around the neck, not caring when he drenches me.

When I finally stand up, once again we are surrounded by a crowd.

Rigel drops the soaked toy at my feet. I hold it up, starting to hear the voices of the crowd around me.

'What a marvellous animal!'

'Should have left it there – stopping the liner for a dog? Never heard the like of it.'

'If I miss my appointment because of this, I'll be expecting compensation from Cunard.'

'At least we know the lifeboats work.'

'Now that's what you call a dog, not one of those handbag pooches . . .'

Then a squeal and the little girl Yolanda emerges, dragging her mother behind her. I hand the toy back to her and her face straightens for a moment as she hugs it tight, soaking her dress. When she holds it up, her face crumples even further than before.

Rigel gives a huge shake, soaking everyone around us, and it's only then I see the little girl's toy rabbit has the stuffing spilling from its face and only one eye.

Old Mrs Palmer slots a firm arm in mine. I remember how she grabbed Mr Chan to send for help so I don't say a word as she leads me and my stupid, shaggy, dripping and very brave friend back to our cabin for another 'restorative lie-down'.

I decide it might be best to keep Rigel out of the way for a bit. Luckily his sea swim seems to have taken the energy out of him and he is happy to flop out on my bed. It's soon time for another meal, although I'm not particularly hungry. For most passengers the ship is a giant floating all-day restaurant.

After dinner I'm forced to join the Palmers and their circle of acquaintances to hear hits from Broadway performed by the ship's band. There's no opportunity for me to get away, in the middle of a row sandwiched between Mrs Palmer and Bernie. Bernie also sat opposite me at dinner and I kept catching her looking at me when she thought I couldn't see her.

It's after half eleven when I finally get back to the cabin and I'm afraid Rigel might have been barking, but everyone in first class seemed to have been at the same recital so I suppose at least he won't have upset anyone. As I open the cabin door, I wonder which cabin is Yolanda and John's and particularly their mother's, hoping it is at the far end of the corridor.

Rigel greets me at the door, flicking his tail like a pennant so his whole body waggles, big black eyes sparkling. The comforter is on the floor and the pillow dumped on top, a few feathers floating in the air. Looks like I've got back just in time – before he got so bored he started to make a colossal mess. I remember Peg as a puppy; I'd forgotten to walk her one day when the others were at market, and she'd torn one of Ma's cookbooks into tiny shreds that filled the whole kitchen.

'Come on, boy,' I say, 'you've been very patient, now let's get you out of here.'

I dress for the cold – remembering how frozen I'd been the night before. I add a cardigan and Gramma's shawl crossed at my shoulders and tied at the back, and pull on woollen stockings. Along with the extra bits I found before in the pockets of Bernie's overcoat: the knitted woollen beret and a pair of fingerless gloves, I'm bundled up good and proper.

The decks are quiet, the cold spiking through my clothes, but this time I'm more warmly wrapped and prepared for it. Tonight there is no moon at all, even the sliver has disappeared, but the stars are like pinpricks in a curtain of thick velvet spread across the night sky, the sea glossy and strange beneath it. Rigel walks beside me, nose to the ground, stopping me short every time he finds a particularly interesting smell. It must be strange to have a dog's senses. I wonder if it's like he's creating a picture with his nose, maybe like Bernie's photographs but made out of . . . scent.

I pass through the gate on to the second-class deck and right to the back of the ship and suddenly my eyes are at the hut where Harry said he works. The lights are on.

He did say I could see how his instruments work. At least he won't be busy with passengers sending messages at this time.

'Come in,' is the curt reply to my knock.

I push open the door to find a small cabin containing a huge array of polished brass equipment, clocks, pipes and dials, more than in the motorcar we'd once taken a ride in. My cousin is curled over what must be the Marconi machine, wearing an alarming-looking contraption on his head with two discs covering his ears and a loop between them. He is busy at work, tapping a brass button on a small machinery box in a strange rhythm, so fast his finger seems to blur. Then he writes something down on a note.

'Yes?' he says briskly, without turning as he puts the note on a pile and fetches a fresh sheet.

'Sorry,' I say, suddenly shy to see my cousin so hard at work and serious, 'I can see you are hard at it, I'll come back another time.'

'Clara?' he says and spins around, frowning and smiling at the same time. He looks me up and down, eyes alighting on the dog and then rolling, but with a proper smile this time. 'I don't know why I'm surprised at you dropping in on me at nearly midnight. I hear you are the reason the ship had to stop. Quite a few of the crew are flummoxed why a renowned captain should take such an interest in a mutt and a stowaway,' he says with the cheeky grin I know so well from my favourite cousin.

I grin and shrug. 'Rigel and I made some friends,' I say – thinking of the captain, possibly of Mrs Palmer who certainly enjoyed showing the stowaway off at mealtimes, and Yolanda and John, then Yolanda's crumpled face and Bernie crouching over her dented camera, 'but possibly some enemies too—'

'Don't tell me – Mr Greeve-Birtwistle? Not afraid to voice his opinions, that one. And a panicking mother is apparently spreading the word that a monstrous bear-like dog almost gulped her baby down whole.'

I sigh. 'Bet she didn't mention Rigel risked his life to save her daughter's toy?'

Harry ruffles Rigel's head. 'Don't worry, cousin, you somehow seem to have the support of the captain, so all will be well.'

'So this is your Marconi machine,' I say, suddenly a little in awe of the complicated equipment. We don't have electricity at home and still use gas lamps and candles. The lamps on the *Carpathia* seem so bright to me. Frank often talks about how annoying it is that the ranch is so far from the main electricity cable, but Ma and Pa are relieved as they don't trust it.

Harry yawns, excuses himself and nods, thumbing through a pile of messages on slips of paper like the one he had written on. 'Yes. The messages are sent out from the shore and from any ships in the area of around two hundred and fifty to three hundred miles, and then I can relay messages back to them.'

I try to imagine how far three hundred miles is. New York City is nearly a hundred miles from the ranch, and that has always seemed like an awful long way to me.

'The messages can travel that far – with no cables to travel along like electricity?'

'Yes. It's a sort of electricity, but it travels through

waves in the air. It can go even further at night, although I couldn't quite explain to you why. When you put it like that it does seem quite fantastical,' he says, rubbing his eyes, 'but it doesn't feel so exciting when you are sending and receiving hundreds a day, and listening to thousands more that have nothing to do with you.'

I frown. 'So you sit there and listen and when there's a message for you, you write it down . . . except you have to translate it from the Morse code dots and dashes? How do you know who the message is for? What sort of things do they say?'

He explains that the private messages are mainly from first-class passengers to shore – maybe contacting friends or booking a hotel – as marconigrams are very expensive.

Then there are more important official messages sharing information between ships.

'For example, I've taken a few messages earlier today about icebergs, growlers and field ice,' he says, reading from a slip of paper.

9. 12 A.M. 14TH APRIL
FROM: CARONIA
TO: TITANIC

CAPTAIN TITANIC WESTBOUND STEAMERS
REPORT BERGS GROWLERS FIELD ICE –
BARR

```
1.26 P.M.  14TH APRIL
FROM: TITANIC
TO: CARONIA


THANKS FOR MESSAGE AND INFORMATION
HAVE HAD VARIABLE WEATHER
THROUGHOUT - SMITH
```

'Smith and Barr are the captains,' says Harry.

'What's a growler?' I say.

'It's a smaller iceberg, one that is less than three feet above the surface. They are usually about the size of a grand piano.'

'Wow – will we get to see some?' I ask. So much to tell Frank and the others.

'Well it's the wrong time of year for icebergs, really,' says Harry, turning back to his machine.

UNITED STATES SENATE INQUIRY

SENATOR BOURNE: Welcome back, Mr Daniels. We will begin where we left off yesterday. Where were you when RMS Titanic hit the iceberg? What did you notice first?

- I was in my bed, just about to fall asleep when the ship gave an almighty judder.

SENATOR BOURNE: What time was this?

- It was about 11.40 Titanic time, the night of the 14th of April.

SENATOR BOURNE: Please give us a complete and full account of your movements and observations from this moment.

- Well - there was the judder, and a groaning sound along with it. The boys mostly woke, but some said it was nothing and rolled over to go back to sleep. A few didn't even stir, it wasn't that powerful. But it also wasn't nothing. And after that the engines sounded . . . wrong to me.

SENATOR BOURNE: Could you be more precise -

what do you mean by wrong?

- The engine was usually like a constant buzz or rumble, but suddenly I felt grinding. I wondered if the ship was turning, even stopping? A group of us raced up the stairs and along the corridors before the chief could appear and bark us back to bed. We took the back stairs behind the galley knowing if we met any second- or first-class passengers - scruffy group that we were, so hastily dressed - there'd be all hell to pay. Excuse my language, sir. We burst up on to the deck and found it was littered with huge chunks of ice.

SENATOR BOURNE: And what did you do when you saw this ice?

- There was a moment where we looked at each other in confusion and it seems so odd now, knowing what the ice meant, but we were just a group of young lads all together in the middle of the night, and everyone started kicking chunks of ice around. The ice slid across the deck at such speed, it was a lark to be honest with you, sir, and a goal was hastily established. But these larks stopped before they began, because Freddie Fleet - the lookout I met earlier - dashed through the middle of the game. I raced after him and caught up to find out what he knew.

SENATOR BOURNE: We'll have that conversation verbatim please, Mr Daniels.

- Sorry, sir, I don't know what you mean by verbat—

SENATOR BOURNE: Just try to describe the exact words that passed between you and Frederick Fleet.

- Sorry, sir. Just . . . I do worry about putting words in another fellow's mouth, sir.

SENATOR BOURNE: The inquiry will take that into account, Mr Daniels. But we will require as full an account as possible. How people seemed to you and exactly what you can remember being said.

- Well, Mr Fleet became very serious, but talking quickly. He said, 'There was a huge iceberg. I couldn't see it, there's no moon. We hit it, starboard - think it caused some damage below the waterline.'

One of the boys, I can't remember who, made a joke. 'Didn't do your job very well then, fella. Thought you were the eagle eyes.'

Freddie Fleet's face was pale. 'No waves breaking against it in seas like this - I couldn't see it. There was nothing to see. Then it was there. Too late.'

One of the other stewards laughed, but

Freddie just shook his head a little and charged on past me and down the stairs.

SENATOR BOURNE: Thank you, Mr Daniels, continue please.

- Well, I didn't feel like larking about after talking to Freddie. I ran to the rail and peered behind me into the dark, seeing if I could catch a glimpse of the iceberg, because the steamer had slowed right down. I called out 'There.' A dark mass was behind us, bigger than a house, blocking out the stars. The rest of the boys fell quiet as we lined along the rail staring at the giant mass that had collided with the Titanic.

SENATOR BOURNE: In your own words describe exactly what you saw. No detail too small.

- It was . . . a mountain of ice with two peaks. The ship had now slowed down so much it was barely moving and you'd expect it to roll side to side when the engines stop but there was nothing. It was strange how still the sea was.

I said to the others: 'Look, there's no waves, that's what the lookout meant. The foam at the base of the ice would normally be easy to see, even on such a dark night.'

The other boys were also staring at the berg and there was talking but I couldn't tell you who said what 'cos my eyes were stuck fast to that iceberg. But it went something like:

'Do you think she's slowed down because there's more of them?'

'Probably normal to find bergs on this crossing - the captain will have it all under control.'

'Don't know what that Fleet was getting so worked up about.'

We all fell quiet until our boss arrived.

SENATOR BOURNE: And who was your boss, Mr Daniels?

- Mr Kieran, sir. Chief Steward Kieran Third Class. He liked us just to call him Chief.

SENATOR BOURNE: Thank you. Go on.

- Mr Kieran said, 'There you are, lads. I need you downstairs now, check on your section and keep the passengers in their berths. Reassure them there is no need for concern. Last thing we need is hysteria. We will not be mentioning icebergs.'

We asked him what we should say then.

Like Freddie, the chief steward's expression didn't fit with what I knew of him - all the boys thought him one of the best you could work for, although he didn't take any nonsense. But his voice was pinched, and I didn't think it just from the cold.

'You tell anyone you see that all is well, but Captain requests all passengers remain in their cabins.'

- No, not quite, sir. I hung back with the chief when the others went back below deck.

I said, 'Is it true though? That all is well?'

Mr Kieran said: 'Mr Andrews himself is down in the engine rooms checking it over. We're travelling with all the experts on board. You just do your job, sonny, and leave the worrying to the big cheeses, those that's paid for it.'

I asked him who Mr Andrews was as I couldn't remember, and he told me he was the ship's designer and no one knew more about the boat.

Then he said: 'Now you strike me as a lad with a good head on your shoulders. Make sure everyone is calm and ready for orders. And thank your lucky stars we hit that beast of a berg with a ship as safe as Titanic.'

Monday

15th

April

1912

12. 15 A.M.
FROM: TITANIC
TO: ALL SHIPS

(RECEIVED BY CAPE RACE)

CQD. REQUIRE ASSISTANCE
41. 46 N 50. 24 W

12. 18 A.M.
FROM: TITANIC
TO: ALL SHIPS

(RECEIVED BY SS YPIRANGA)

CQD. REQUIRE ASSISTANCE
41. 44 N 50. 24 W

Harry takes the contraption off his head and holds it out to me.

I am about to put it on my head when something occurs to me. 'But the electricity comes through here . . .'

'Don't worry about that.' He points to a large wall panel covered in knobs and dials. 'The electricity is converted to sounds in the headset. I'm not fried am I? Go on, take a listen, it's perfectly safe. Aunt would never forgive me if I electrocuted my youngest cousin.'

I flinch a little as I place the headset over my ears. My skull is immediately filled with sound and despite everything I know I'm surprised not to hear voices, just chains of beeps and longer beeps tapped out in streams of rhythm.

I take the headset off, shaking my head. 'It's so fast! How do you catch it all, there's no time to check the code sheet like you sent me, is there?'

He shook his head. 'You have to learn what the dots and dashes mean like a language, and you can't do this job until you are fluent. Definitely no code sheet. But even then I sometimes miss things.' Harry rubs his eyes. 'Which reminds me, I've been asking for a confirmation of a message from another boat, the *Parisian*. Earlier I couldn't make it out – happens a lot. Although I started work at eight a.m. so really I'm only fit for bed.'

He puts the headset back on but only covers one ear.

I'm fascinated that my cousin has been listening and translating this beep-pause-beep language for – I do the math – sixteen hours. Makes me feel lazy.

'Where do you sleep, then?' I ask.

Harry turns in his spinning chair and pushes open the door to a small cabin with only one bunk. 'Just through there, so I'm close to the equipment. I'm the only Marconi operator on board so can't go far. On a bigger ship they have more than one and can take proper shifts.'

What a responsibility, and he's not even as old as Frank.

'While I'm waiting for this message to come through, can you read some of those out to me?' he says, handing me a pile of slips.

I perch on the edge of his desk and do as he asks, proud to be helping, as he taps out the messages from the *Carpathia* passengers. I marvel at the speed he strikes the button, sending the Morse code out across the ocean.

Then he stops, frowning, and holds up a hand.

'Speaking of bigger ships, there's a whole load of messages waiting for the *Titanic* at Cape Cod – that's the shore station,' he says. 'My pals Harold Bride and Jack Phillips are her wireless operators – we were on Marconi training together. I'll see if I can get through.'

He pauses, then begins tapping out a message to his old pals:

12.25 A.M. 15TH APRIL
FROM: CARPATHIA
TO: TITANIC

GOOD MORNING OLD MAN. DO YOU KNOW
THERE ARE MESSAGES WAITING FOR YOU
AT CAPE COD?

Head down, Harry starts tapping again and then his face drains of all colour. He snatches up one of the blank telegraph slips, saying the words quietly aloud as he writes what he must be hearing.

```
12.25 A.M.
FROM: TITANIC
TO: ALL SHIPS

CQD
SOS

12.25 A.M.
FROM: TITANIC
TO: CARPATHIA

IT'S A CQD. COME AT ONCE. WE HAVE
STRUCK A BERG. IT'S A CQD OLD MAN.
POSITION 41.46 N 50.14 W
```

Harry hunches over, tapping again as I try to take it in. Can he actually have said the *Titanic* has struck a berg? Does that mean iceberg? What are the chances of that when we were just talking about them? Lucky it's such a big ship.

'I've asked *Titanic* if I should tell the captain,' says

Harry, 'and all he replied was, "Yes. Come Quick."'

I gasp. 'What does CQD mean, Harry?'

'CQ means calling all ships. D stands for distress. Means there's an emergency, it is the distress call.'

He hands a sheet of paper to me and then pauses as if unsure. 'Can I trust you, Clara, to take this and give it to no one but Captain Rostron? I don't want to leave my post in case anything else comes through from *Titanic*. Anyone stops you, tell them it's an urgent Marconi message.'

I take the slip of paper, clutching it tight in my hand. 'You can trust me, I'll take it right now.'

I meet Harold's eyes.

'Can you really do this, Clara, promise me absolutely no—'

'—antics,' I finish, looking down at the floor. 'I promise.'

Harry gives me a concerned look and a curt nod before hunching back over the machine.

STORY IN PICTURE OF HOW WIRELESS WAKED THE MIDNIGHT SEA

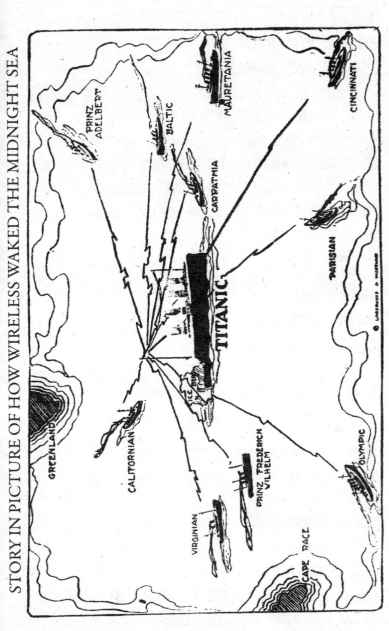

17th April 1912 *The Day Books of Chicago*

12.26 A.M.
FROM: TITANIC
TO: SS YPIRANGA

CQD. HERE CORRECTED POSITION
41.46 N 50.14 W
REQUIRE IMMEDIATE ASSISTANCE.
WE HAVE COLLISION WITH ICEBERG.
SINKING. CAN HEAR NOTHING FOR
NOISE OF STEAM

12.27 A.M.
FROM: TITANIC
TO: ALL SHIPS

I REQUIRE ASSISTANCE IMMEDIATELY.
STRUCK BY ICEBERG IN 41.46 N 50.14 W

12.30 A.M.
FROM: TITANIC
TO: FRANKFURT

CQD SOS
TELL YOUR CAPTAIN TO COME TO OUR
HELP WE ARE ON THE ICE

27

I clutch the message Harry received from *Titanic* and race along the second-class promenade past the towering funnel. Icy air cuts into my cheeks, making my eyes run even though I'm hot beneath all the woollen layers. Rigel's rope is in my other hand and he trots alongside me. The sound of that humming tap of the Marconi machine is still in my ears as I pass through the gate on to the first-class promenade. I've seen an officer guarding this gate in the day but am relieved no one is here now, I guess because it's so late at night.

The bridge is just forward of the first-class dining

room, when I see it rising out of the deck, I slow to a walk.

A man steps in front of me. I've never seen him before, but recognize the long navy frockcoat and gold buttons of an officer's uniform.

'Miss Scott,' says the officer, folding his arms and blocking my way. 'I can't allow you any further. The majority of the passengers have already retired.'

I frown. This young officer knows my name, but I've never seen him before. There's something familiar about him. Round eyes and a very small nose for his face, just . . . like my old friend Mr Greeve-Birtwistle! I remember Mr Chan warning me about the steward's son, the third officer.

I raise my chin. He's heard of me, but I've also heard of him. 'Officer Greeve-Birtwistle. I have an urgent message for the captain, a telegraph message from the Marconi room.'

The officer tilts his head to one side, peering at me. 'It's just Greeve. Urgent communications are always delivered in person by Mr Cottam,' he says, mouth folded so tight it's like he's sucking a sherbet pip. He doesn't move to let me by.

Burying my gloved hand deep in Rigel's neck fur, I square my shoulders.

'This is a CQD distress signal, *sir*. Harold Cottam is

my cousin and he's busy contacting all ships in the area. He can't leave his post and he trusted me to get this message to the captain.'

I try to pass him but he moves to block my way. Rigel releases a low growl.

'Well, more fool Cottam. I will take the telegram to Captain Rostron myself,' he says, holding out his hand for the slip of paper. His jaw clenches when I don't hand it over.

Cousin Harry said to deliver the message in person and that is what I am going to do.

'I don't mean to be rude but you aren't the captain, are you? This is a distress call from *Titanic* and I am the one who has been asked to deliver it.'

The officer laughs and the sound isn't kind. 'The *Titanic*? I don't know what you are up to, child, but I've heard tell of your capers with that animal. Now hand it over.'

I remember how urgent Harry said this message is. So when Third Officer Greeve swipes at my hand as if to snatch the letter, I duck, then dart forward, willing to barge past him if I have to. Rigel slips from my grasp on the rope and leaps up at the man with a low growl. The officer is so surprised he loses balance and falls against the rails sideways, and then hits the deck.

I take my opportunity and run as fast as I can, Rigel

and his trailing leash behind me. I burst into the cabin at the front of the ship, the dog skittering to a halt across the floor. A couple of other officers sit at a large, curved desk.

'I have a message for the captain,' I pant.

One of the men holds out his hand with a grim glare, but I've had enough of this.

'Captain! Captain Rostron!' I yell with all my might and the last of my breath. The men start towards me as the captain emerges from a flight of stairs I hadn't noticed.

'What is the meaning of—'

'Captain,' I sigh in relief as I thrust the note into his hand. 'CQD from the *Titanic*, sir.'

The two officers scowl at each other. The captain reads and then speaks in a low voice.

'Has Mr Cottam confirmed assistance is needed . . .?'

Officer Greeve bursts into the room. 'My apologies, Captain. I tried to prevent this interruption—'

'Silence, Greeve,' snaps the captain. Third Officer Greeve's face flushes so red I almost feel sorry for him. Almost.

I turn my back to him and continue. I remember Harry's expression, his trust in me. I need to get this right.

'Yes, sir, I heard Harry – Mr Cottam – ask if he

should tell the captain, and the *Titanic* replied yes, come at once.'

Captain Rostron paces two steps in one direction, two steps in the other.

The captain turns to me first. 'Thank you, Miss Scott. Johns, run to Mr Cottam personally. Message for *Titanic* – "Please confirm coordinates; we are fifty-eight miles away and coming with all haste".'

The captain then gives orders for the two officers to alter the course.

Somehow I can't move. The captain seems so stressed and serious. A ship as huge, grand and brand new as the *Titanic* can't be in serious trouble, can it?

'Take this down, Greeve,' said the captain. 'Have coffee, tea, soup, et cetera, in each saloon, blankets in saloons, at the gangways, and some for the boats. My cabin and all officials' cabins to be given up to *Titanic* passengers if needed. Smoke rooms, library, et cetera, dining rooms, will be utilized as accommodation.'

The officers' mouths drop open, but the captain continues rattling off, 'Company rockets to be fired every quarter hour. Fetch me the doctor, the purser and the chief steward, immediately. All steam must be diverted from heating the cabins, as we will need all power to get us to *Titanic*'s position in a timely fashion.'

Another man arrives at the door, flustered, wearing a

different dark uniform. He glances uncertainly at me and Rigel before the captain turns to greet him.

'Sir, I got the message something was amiss?'

'The *Titanic* is calling distress, requiring immediate assistance.' Captain Rostron points to the charts in front of him. 'I need the efforts of your entire department. At normal cruising speed we'd require four hours to get to her. We need to be there much quicker in the event we are the only ship answering the call. All shifts of trimmers and stokers to report for duty immediately.'

The two men discuss a couple of other particulars I don't understand until finally Rigel and I are alone with Captain Rostron.

The captain mutters to himself: 'We'll need canvas ash bags to be at each gangway, for lifting up the children from the lifeboats.'

I can't believe what I am hearing. Bags for the children? My voice comes out small.

'But I heard them say at dinner that the *Titanic* is the biggest liner in the world. That it is unsinkable, sir.'

Just when I think Captain Rostron hasn't heard me he says, 'No ship is unsinkable, Miss Scott.'

12.36 A.M.
FROM: TITANIC
TO: PRINZ FRIEDRICH WILHELM

ARE YOU COMING TO OUR

12.36 A.M.
FROM: TITANIC
TO: FRANKFURT

WE HAVE COLLISION WITH ICEBERG.
SINKING. PLEASE TELL CAPTAIN TO
COME

UNITED STATES SENATE INQUIRY

Day 10 - 28th April 1912
Testimony of Sidney Daniels

SENATOR BOURNE: Please continue your account, Mr Daniels. Every detail of your experience, none is too small. If you need to take some water or use the restroom at any time, please do so. The inquiry recognizes this testimony may be distressing to you.

- Thank you, sir. After I spoke to the chief, I joined the other stewards back below in our sections and honestly, my chat with the chief left me none too concerned. All was as it should be in our corridor. When I advised one of the passengers to return to his bed, he did so willingly.

SENATOR BOURNE: What time was this, Mr Daniels? For the record.

- I can't say exactly, sir, but must have been well past midnight by then.

SENATOR BOURNE: And at that time the third-class passengers were still in their cabins?

- They were, sir. Then Mr Kieran came back. He gathered us in our little mess area next to the linen cupboard to allocate tasks.

- The first thing he said was, 'I need all of you to put on these life jackets. Whatever happens, don't take them off.'

We asked if it was a drill.

He said it wasn't and carried on, 'I haven't been told much, but it turns out Mr Andrews is unhappy with some of the damage to the hull. So he's being cautious,' he said and, sounding disgruntled, 'of course it's easy to be cautious and give orders when you aren't the one carrying them out, but that's between you and me, my boys.'

So we pulled the bulky pale canvas life jackets over our heads, and helped each other with the ties around the waist.

Mr Kieran allocated most of the lads to wake the passengers, ask them to put their life jackets on and then tell them to wait for further instructions. The lads grumbled under their breaths at this order and I understood why. Many of the men in my section barely spoke English, and we would have a job communicating something we didn't understand ourselves. Asking folks to pop on a life jacket was sure to get them lathered up.

He asked six of us to stay back and I was

one of them.

'You fellows are needed on the deck,' he said. 'Report to an officer when you get up there.' Then he clapped us each on the shoulder.

Up on deck I felt like I'd stepped into one of those strange dreams, the sort I'd had in the nights before leaving home to go aboard. Except this was real. The huge ship Titanic wasn't made to be unmoving, still as the sea that night. Music flooded the air and some were already on deck, like it was daytime, but it was the middle of the night.

The musicians played like it was a midnight ball, jolly jazz numbers, and while I was waiting for orders me and a couple of the other lads even had a little . . . well, we had a little dance. We didn't know where we were supposed to be.

SENATOR BOURNE: So would you describe the mood as cheerful?

- Not exactly, sir. But we never imagined what was going to happen, not even close. We was dancing because we didn't know what else to do. We were nervy, I think. And to be honest sir, we didn't usually get to hear the band down in third class.

12.45 A.M.
FROM: TITANIC
TO: OLYMPIC

SOS

12.50 A.M.
FROM: TITANIC
TO: ALL SHIPS

(RECEIVED BY CELTIC)

I REQUIRE IMMEDIATE ASSISTANCE.
POSITION 41.46 N 50.14 W

UNITED STATES SENATE INQUIRY

Day 10 - 28th April 1912
Testimony of Sidney Daniels

SENATOR BOURNE: So at this time the crew had no knowledge that the ship would founder?

- I couldn't say, sir. But I doubt it.

Seems like blasphemy to say it, but we was almost excited about what was going to happen next. Sorry, sir.

SENATOR BOURNE: You weren't to know, Daniels. Continue.

- Finally two officers arrived, quietened the band and put a stop to the high spirits. Up until that moment I expected them to say that us being called to deck had been a drill, or a mistake. That Titanic would be continuing on its way shortly.

But one of them raised his voice and when everyone on this side of the deck could hear him, he said, 'My name is Officer Moody and this is Officer Murdoch, we are in charge of loading the lifeboats from the starboard side of the ship. It's us you will need to listen to - take no order from anyone else. I am glad you lads are keeping your pecker up, but let's take it down a few notches now. The

women and children will be coming up shortly
and we will need an attitude of calm to get
them away safely.'

I looked at the fellow who now stood next
to me, an older chap with the blackened hands
and face of a fireman. I thought it was mighty
strange that he was up here on deck. He raised
his eyebrows which were bushy and reminded me
of my da's. Moody directed me and this chap to
the same lifeboat, number 13.

The other stewards I was with were sent to
other boats.

Moody's words began to sink in.

The women and children were going to be put
in lifeboats. I remember looking at the sea,
so dark and so far down, and thinking it
wouldn't really happen.

SENATOR BOURNE: Had the demeanour of the crew
changed on deck at this point?

- Yes, sir. It went quiet, people moving to
where they were told. The band started playing again but not such jolly numbers.

I got talking to the fireman. He asked me
if I was superstitious, pointing at the
number 13 painted in black on the white slats
of the lifeboat.

'No, sir,' I said, and offered my hand.
'Sid Daniels, third-class steward.'

'Frederick Barratt, lead stoker,' he said.

The stokers were the strong men of the ship,

spending all day shovelling coal to power the huge engines. If there was damage to the ship I guessed this fellow might know about it.

'Is everything all right . . . well - I mean, below with the engines, Mr Barratt?' I said.

I felt he was on the brink of telling me something but then he started surveying the lifeboat, knocking his knuckles against the white painted slats, and gave me no answer.

But something answered the question for me. A beam of light shot into the air, exploding in a burst of white stars. Another from the other side.

Titanic was sending out signal flares. Barratt and I watched but he wouldn't meet my eyes.

It was then a lot of the crew realized things were not well with the ship, sir; they were looking at each other, shifting, nervous. But if they knew how bad it was they never showed it.

SENATOR BOURNE: Go on when you are ready, Mr Daniels.

- Yes, sir. Mr Barratt said to me: 'You're a friendly-looking lad, Daniels. You just keep the ladies and little 'uns calm and do as your elders tell you to. All right, sonny? And it's just Barratt.'

I nodded as there was noises from the stair-well and the first passengers arrived, bundled

- 194 -

in blankets but some still in their nightwear, some even in evening dress. The lifeboat which looked quite large up on deck suddenly seemed too small, as it hit me that the officers were actually going to load women and children that far down the side of the ship.

Off the Titanic in the middle of the ocean.

In the night.

In the dark.

In the freezing cold.

It seemed impossibly dangerous.

SENATOR BOURNE: Why did you think that, Mr Daniels?

- Well - the Titanic was awful tall, sir? Like a building, like one of those big New York buildings and everything was pitch-black with no moon.

The only way this made sense was if it would be more dangerous to stay on board than to leave. And I couldn't believe that, sir, I don't think anyone could.

The wait was long, at our posts beside the lifeboats, the canvas covers off and the women and children emerging up the stairs.

I saw Captain Smith pass by twice, which is more than I'd seen him on the whole journey. I kept expecting him or one of the officers to call out that it was a drill, a false alarm, back to our beds.

But of course, no one did.

1.00 A.M.
FROM: TITANIC
TO: OLYMPIC

POSITION 41.46 N 50.14 W
WE HAVE STRUCK AN ICEBERG

1.02 A.M.
FROM: TITANIC
TO: ASIAN

WANT IMMEDIATE ASSISTANCE

1.10 A.M.
FROM: TITANIC
TO: OLYMPIC

WE ARE IN COLLISION WITH A BERG.
SINKING HEAD DOWN. 41.46 N 50.14 W.
COME SOON AS POSSIBLE

28

Me and Rigel are still waiting by the door in the bridge, unnoticed, as Captain Rostron barks more orders.

'I will post extra lookouts in the crow's nest but will need my best eyes stationed at the bow and bridge wing. Watch for lights, flares and most of all ice. I will have every ounce of your effort and concentration for this mission.'

'What is the status of the berg that *Titanic* hit? Do we know if it is still in the area or if there are others?' says one of the officers.

'To reach *Titanic* we will be skirting the edge of an unseasonable ice field at the very least,' says Captain Rostron. 'We may even have to pass through it.'

I see one of the officers twist his hands behind his back; another's mouth drops open and quickly snaps shut again. The captain dips his chin, his voice low.

'Of course *Carpathia*'s passengers' safety is paramount, but we can't in all good conscience ignore this call. The *Titanic* is requesting immediate assistance. We may be the only ship to reach the area in time. Even then – our journey may take upwards of four hours.'

Silence.

The officers acknowledge their orders and quickly disperse.

I swallow. The passengers of the *Carpathia* are in danger too. We're going to steam through an ice field in the middle of the night.

I want to talk to the captain but he is consulting charts and I decide to slip from the bridge without disturbing him. I start back towards first class, Rigel at my side, feeling the vibration of the increased engine power through the deck. I can't go back to Harry, he will be incredibly busy now, but I also can't imagine sleeping. We walk slowly, me staring out to sea, Rigel looking up at me every few moments. He senses something is wrong. I know this is a very serious accident and lives are at risk, but that doesn't mean I can believe it. Instead I'm keen to see an iceberg, eager to be involved in the rescue of the *Titanic* passengers. I wonder how many there are. Thousands? I'm so distracted I almost bump into Mr Greeve-Birtwistle. I roll my eyes.

'All passengers to stay in their berths, captain's orders,' snaps the chief steward. Rigel clearly likes his tone of voice as much as I do. Up in the bridge the dog was so quiet and well behaved no one noticed him. Now he growls.

I feel like asking why the first-class chief steward doesn't have more important things to worry about than bossing us around – but decide it isn't wise.

'Just on my way now, Mr Greeve-Birtwistle,' I say sweetly.

Then I really don't have much choice but to do as he says, as he follows me until we enter the first-class cabin corridor. He peers around the corner, checking as I let us into my cabin. I snuggle up with Rigel, fully clothed, thinking about all I've heard and planning to sneak back out on deck when Greeve-Birtwistle has gone.

1.25 A.M.
FROM: CARONIA
TO: TITANIC

BALTIC COMING TO YOUR ASSISTANCE

1.25 A.M.
FROM: OLYMPIC
TO: TITANIC

POSITION 40.52 N 61.18 W. ARE YOU
STEERING SOUTHERLY TO MEET US?

1.25 A.M.
FROM: TITANIC
TO: OLYMPIC

WE ARE PUTTING THE WOMEN OFF IN THE
BOATS

1.30 A.M.
FROM: TITANIC
TO: OLYMPIC

WE ARE PUTTING PASSENGERS OFF IN
SMALL BOATS. CLEAR AND CALM.

UNITED STATES SENATE INQUIRY

SENATOR BOURNE: You said earlier you saw Captain Smith, but did you hear any more from the captain as you mustered at your positions?

- Yes, sir, he spoke to us over the loudhailer.

He said, 'This is your captain speaking. Lifeboats, remain close by, wait for further orders.'

It was followed by a hoot from the ship's funnel.

I'd thought that might be a good sign. The captain probably wanted the lifeboats to stay close to Titanic because he expected whatever problem there was with the ship to soon be solved.

SENATOR BOURNE: You still had no idea the ship was sinking?

- No, sir. I didn't believe it and no one said that was what was happening. Mr Moody and Murdoch started to load and launch the lifeboats one by one. We watched as the first three boats on this side of the ship were launched.

SOLICITOR GENERAL: Had you taken part in a lifeboat drill since the ship left port?

- No, sir. I did hear a drill was planned for Sunday the 14th but was cancelled as Captain Smith wanted a religious service instead.

SOLICITOR GENERAL: Please describe the lifeboat launch in as much detail as you remember.

- Well, the first launches weren't all that smooth to be honest with you, sir, anyone will tell you that. The boats swung out from the side of the ship and the officers didn't seem fully in control of the davits - the pulleys, where the ropes were attached - although I'm sure they must have known what they was doing. There were yelps of fear from the passengers.

But when the first boat of women and children rowed clear of the Titanic into the dark I remember how quiet it was as everyone watched. The only men on board those first lifeboats were a couple of sailors there for the rowing. I didn't envy them at the time.

SENATOR BOURNE: Please go on.

- Well, watching the first lifeboat row out of sight seemed to change the feeling up there on deck. More passengers had come up from below and some started to argue with each other. A man who had been waiting by number 13 with me tried to put his wife and baby on to the next lifeboat instead.

'I'll join you on one of the later boats,' he said.

'I'm not going anywhere without you. I can't!' she said, all low, like she didn't want to be noticed.

The man held her close, whispering into her hair. I looked away out at where the first lifeboat had disappeared into the dark. It was soon to be joined by another that must have been launched from the other side of the ship. The second was only half full which made me frown. When I looked back, the woman was on the next boat with her baby, tears streaming down her face.

I didn't know where the lifeboats were going, what was really happening, no one seemed to.

SENATOR BOURNE: So when did you realize Titanic was sinking?

- I know exactly when, sir. I do.

There was a kid holding tight to the hand of his older brother in the queue for the lifeboat next to ours and he dropped something. It rolled towards me, gathering pace. A marble.

I stopped it with my boot, unable to take in what the speeding roll of the marble meant as I picked it up. By then the little boy was gone, dragged away by his family to load on to the next lifeboat.

It was green glass with a red dash inside like an eye.

SOLICITOR GENERAL: If we could get back to when you first gathered the boat was sinking.

- Yes, sir. I am. See - I used to play marbles myself with the other kids in the schoolyard or the lane behind our terrace. And a marble only rolled like that on a proper slope.

That was when I realized I could feel it in the muscles at my calves. The Titanic was tilted.

I had a lot of thoughts then, a lot of things rushed in on me at once but one kept rising to the top.

Could the Titanic actually be sinking?

Everything suggested it, the lifeboats, flares . . .

Sounds daft now, but I know I wasn't the only one who just could not imagine it.

I tried to make myself imagine the ship sinking and what would happen to me or the other lads. I couldn't. It was like there was a blank space where that thought would go.

I decided I would stay at my post until the work was done and the ladies and kids were in the lifeboats. I was crew on the Titanic and I knew my duty.

1. 35 A.M.
FROM: TITANIC
TO: ALL SHIPS

ENGINE ROOM GETTING FLOODED

1. 37 A.M.
FROM: BALTIC
TO: TITANIC

WE ARE RUSHING TO YOU

I'm just about defrosted when Rigel springs from where we are curled together, almost knocking me off the bed.

'What is it Rigel?'

He stands, ears cocked, head tilted, then leaps back up and over me.

'What are you doing, dog?' I say, then see the port-hole behind my head. The iron door on the round window is closed and I flip it up on to its catch. Rigel's fluffy hair is in my face, his growls and yaps in my ear, as we both peer out, and at first I can't make out a thing in the darkness. There is no moon and although the sky is peppered with stars, they don't provide enough light to even reflect off the sea. It is only when some of the scattered stars are blocked that I make out an outline, a shadow – and a huge iceberg, tall as a building, passes by.

Iceberg. I'm looking at an actual iceberg.

As far as I can see the sky and sea are blotched with these darker areas, some scattered with the tiniest glints that must be the reflection of stars – or maybe the lights from the ship – on their icy surface. I remember the captain said the ship lights would all be turned low to save power that could be used to go faster.

I've been shushing Rigel's yaps and growls without thinking, but now he sets up loud determined barks, almost like a slowed-down version of Morse code.

That's the bark Rigel gave when he sensed the sea serpent. I stare out again, but there's no chance of making anything out in this darkness. Rigel looks from me to the porthole and back again with wide, frustrated eyes. Eyes that can see better than mine. It couldn't be clearer that he's telling me something.

With coat and boots back on, I secure the rope to a jumpy barking Rigel and head into the corridor. I crouch in front of the dog, holding his huge chops so he looks at me.

'Settle down,' I whisper firmly. 'Quiet, Rigel.'

Rigel whines once and pants, floppy ears twitching, but he does stop barking this time.

The captain said if Rigel detected the sea serpent to go straight to him. Would he still want that, even now his ship has such an urgent mission?

For once no one stops me on my way to the bridge, and the ship's lights have been turned low so I can slip in and out of the shadows more easily. Besides, every member of the crew is busy carrying out the long list of orders from the captain. Stewards carry bundles of towels and blankets, the steamer chairs that had been stowed for the night are dragged into rows on the deck. I'm sure even more is going on inside; as I pass the huge first-class saloon noting the lights are on, the chairs have been cleared to one end and mattresses line the floors in rows. It makes me think of a hospital ward.

Sure, the *Titanic* passengers will be scared, and cold, but they won't be injured if they are in lifeboats, will they? I try to imagine us pulling alongside the giant broken-down steamer but can't picture it.

The boat deck of *Carpathia* is a hive of activity but with no passengers in sight. I have to give it to him, Mr Greeve-Birtwistle is doing a very good job of keeping everyone in their cabins and out of the way.

I am almost at the bridge when I experience the first strong sway of the *Carpathia* and topple against the cabin wall. The iceberg only blocks the darkness when the ship has already steered to avoid it. I gasp in air so cold it hurts my chest; our change in path doesn't look nearly enough to avoid a collision. The dark icy mass is like a building travelling towards me at speed – the ship is going to crash right into it. I freeze as we make just enough of a turn.

The cliff of ice slides past the ship, a dark and pitted wall with an otherworldly glimmer to it. It looks like rock, like it shouldn't float, like it shouldn't be possible. It's like no ice I've ever seen, and its shadow slithers over me, chilling.

Fear forgotten, I run to the rail and reach out my hand to touch – but it is out of reach. The air left behind by the passing iceberg smells earthy, mildewy and strange, and I wonder where the chunk of ice actually came from as I finally reach the bridge. I wait in the shadows outside the door and, when another officer comes out, I dart in.

One officer is at the wheel, the captain to one side, eyes glued to the window out of which I see more officers on watch at the prow, shining storm lamps into the sea.

I bite my lip, suddenly unsure. Should I be here? The captain did say to fetch him if Rigel behaved like that again, if he might be signalling the sea serpent is there, but that was before he answered a distress call and started dodging icebergs at high speed in the middle of the night.

One of the officers spots me. 'Miss, I'm going to need to ask you to leave.'

'Miss Scott?' says the captain, then without tearing his eyes from the view in front of him, he barks an order – 'Gently to port, Jones' then beckons to me without turning. I stand at his elbow, holding my breath as another shadow looms to the opposite side of the boat. From here, with the power lamps shining at the sea, I can make out smaller bergs and further out, a layer of ice almost covering the whole sea.

The captain wipes his brow and looks down at me finally, raising his eyebrows.

'It's Rigel, sir, I think he can see what he saw before—'

An officer bursts into the room. 'Message from *Titanic*, Captain.'

'Read.'

```
1.45 A.M.
FROM: TITANIC
TO: CARPATHIA

ENGINE ROOM FULL UP TO BOILERS
```

No one says a thing for a long moment. Maybe the officers are trying to figure out what the message means like I am. Or they know but can't believe it.

If *Titanic* is filling with water, then *Titanic* might be sinking.

'You heard that, our mission just—'

Before I can hear the rest of what the captain has to say, Rigel yanks the cord out of my hand and darts out of the door, barking.

1. 47 A. M.
FROM: TITANIC
TO: ALL SHIPS

SIGNAL UNREADABLE

I find Rigel at the bow of the ship where officers and lookouts are lined along the upturned V of the railings, shining torches out into the ocean.

'Stay at your posts if you are on lookout,' barks one man. 'Every other hand to get ahold of the blasted animal.'

Rigel races to the port side of the railings, springing to rest his paws on the top bar. Just like he did before he leapt into the sea to rescue the little girl's toy.

'No, Rigel!' I scream. I charge across the deck as two men finally catch the dog's collar and try to drag him back along the deck. Rigel struggles, woofing, yapping and now snarling – seems he's desperate to stay where he is, head now through the bars. I finally reach him and grab his head, speaking into his ear.

'It's all right, Rigel, I'm here,' I say.

The two officers don't release his collar.

'Ignore the child and get that animal below deck.' The command is bellowed directly in my ear.

Then suddenly a much calmer voice. Captain Rostron. 'Release the dog,' he says.

'Sir, the animal is distracting the—'

'Release the dog immediately.'

Free of the two men gripping his collar, Rigel's paws spring back up on to the railing and he barks again, the urgent telling-me-something bark. I wrap my arms around his huge neck and place my head next to his. He seems to be staring far out into the distance – where the lamps don't reach and all is inky black.

Where the icebergs are invisible.

'What is it, boy?' Rigel looks at me, then back out to sea, yapping again.

The captain raises his eyeglass. 'Thirty degrees to port! Growler!' he bellows. I see confused looks pass between the officers also holding eyeglasses as well as the powerful lamps.

'Can't see it, sir,' calls out one.

'Thirty degrees port, now!' says the captain and a bell rings.

What are Rigel and the captain both seeing that everybody else isn't?

I think of the sea serpent arrowing towards me and Rigel.

Then Rigel bounces down from the rails and races to the prow of the boat, barking again.

Captain Rostron is right beside him this time, scanning the area where Rigel is looking.

As the ship turns, a wide low iceberg comes into sight. I remember Harry explaining to me what a growler was.

'Watch for a wake at the base of the bergs,' says Captain Rostron to the lookouts. 'There's unusual turbulence giving us early warning.'

More concerned looks pass between the officers but they do as he commands. The back of my neck tingles, my body tense, waiting for us to crash just like the *Titanic*.

'Berg right ahead,' calls one of the lookouts.

Just where Rigel was barking. I can't see a thing, not the telltale patch of black where the iceberg blocks the stars, nothing at all. But it's all action on deck as all the officers realize what they are looking for. The bell rings, in a minute or so there's a grinding vibration and soon the ship veers to the left. I watch the iceberg that was right ahead sail by us, glittering darkly. The officers now seem to wait for Rigel, who soon bounces to one side again, barking.

A few quiet moments from the officers as they scan with their eyeglasses and then a call, the bell, followed by the ponderous swerve of the steamer, just in time.

Can it really be the sea serpent?

Because all I can think is that the giant beast is circling the icebergs in front of us, big enough to make its own waves.

If there is a more reasonable explanation for what Rigel is sensing, I can't think of it. Rigel's eyes might be sharper than ours but him spotting icebergs himself wouldn't account for the times he's detected the sea serpent. No – the waves caused by the beast must be lapping and breaking against the icebergs, so the *Carpathia* is able to navigate these disastrous obstacles towards the *Titanic*.

That's all well and good, but it's the next thought that gives me chills. The creature has the whole ocean to explore, and surely doesn't realize how it's helping navigate.

So what is it here for?

1. 48 A. M.
FROM: TITANIC
TO: ALL SHIPS

SOS

UNITED STATES SENATE INQUIRY

Day 10 - 28th April 1912
Testimony of Sidney Daniels

SENATOR BOURNE: And the general atmosphere at this point as the slope of the deck became apparent?

- Oh, everyone was getting worried now, sir. The band continued to play jaunty dance hall songs interspersed with slower numbers and I think we was all glad of the music. I tried to concentrate on the tunes because every time I tuned into the voices around me the situation became more real; passengers was pleading for officers to allow their husbands on the lifeboats, men was pleading with their wives to leave without them, so many questions for the officers about what was actually happening . . . and minute by minute more panic and fear.

Then it was lifeboat 13's turn to be loaded and that was my job. I was glad to help the women, children and a small handful of men into the boat.

SOLICITOR GENERAL: At this point did there seem to be enough lifeboats for all?

- I honestly hadn't thought about it, sir. I

suppose I presumed there was even then. It was Barratt who made me consider it in the end.

'Ask them to shuffle up, we need to fit in the passengers on deck A below,' said Barratt to another young sailor who was assisting. I peered to where he was pointing to the deck below, where people were also queuing. They would need to climb over the railings as the boat was lowered.

'I don't think it's safe to overload the boat.' The young sailor squared his shoulders and I could see he wasn't keen to contradict the burly older fireman.

Barratt leant in very close to the sailor, pulling me in with him so the passengers couldn't hear.

'Have you taken a look at the number of lifeboats this side of the ship? And the other? Do you know how many souls are on this ship? Well, I'm afraid it doesn't add up.'

As I said before, I'd never given any thought to the lifeboats, let alone how many there were, but if I had — well I would have expected there to be enough. For everyone.

But I immediately knew the fireman was speaking the truth.

I think Barratt saw the shock on our faces because he continued more softly saying, 'Nothing we can do about it, boys. But this lifeboat we are launching . . . it will save as many souls as it can possibly take.'

We got on with the job, loading the

passengers. Officer Moody appeared with
another sailor and ordered Barratt and the
young sailor into the boat.

SENATOR BOURNE: While this was going on, were
there any other signs the ship was in a state
of emergency?

- Yes, sir. Flares had been shooting up regu-
larly, every few minutes I think as this
bluish-white light would illuminate the ship.
I remember as lifeboat 13 filled up, three
flares were set off one after the other.
There was also another announcement by the
captain for the lifeboats to remain close to
the ship.

SENATOR BOURNE: And did they - stay close?

- They did not, sir. Most of the lifeboats had
already rowed off out of sight. And the rest
were following. I didn't know why. But
Barratt gripped my shoulder before he climbed
in number 13. 'See them travelling away from
the ship against captain's orders? It's
because of the suction, they don't want to go
down with her. Stay out of the water, son, and
if you can't do that then swim away from the
ship fast as you can.'

I shuddered at his words. If there weren't
enough lifeboats then I knew . . . but it was
easier not to believe it. I hadn't let myself

even think about going into the sea.

SENATOR BOURNE: Take a sip of water if you need it, Mr Daniels.

- Thank you, sir. So. When we started to lower number 13, the passengers clutched on to each other.

The lights on the ship flashed. The band played, and more and more people swirled up from below deck, queuing for the next lifeboat, peering over the rails, huddling in groups. There were noises then from deep inside the ship, bangs, crashes, even explosions. And bursts of steam.

Now I'd thought of it, I couldn't stop wondering what I was going to do when all the lifeboats had launched. What were all the people who didn't make it aboard a boat going to do? And what about the other stewards, the lads, my friends who might still be way down below in the guts of the ship? I couldn't see any of them or even the third-class passengers I'd recognize from my section. I thought now I'd done my duty I should go find them, but . . .

Sorry, sir, I'm going on a bit, it's just - when it comes back to me, it's like all of it comes back at once.

SENATOR BOURNE: It's all right, son, just take your time.

- Well, as lifeboat 13 hit the water I heard a shriek. I stared down to see lifeboat 13 pushed by a geyser of water being pumped from the ship, and it shot back towards where the next lifeboat was hovering just above the sea.

I yelled 'stop' to the officers, but they were already trying; both Moody and Murdoch and other officers were hauling on the ropes at the davits.

I tried not to look, I could do nothing, and didn't want to see one boat of passengers crush the others or tip them into the freezing sea . . . but I couldn't look away.

1.55 A.M.
FROM: CAPE RACE
TO: VIRGINIAN

WE HAVE NOT HEARD TITANIC FOR ABOUT
HALF AN HOUR.

HIS POWER MAY BE GONE

UNITED STATES SENATE INQUIRY

SENATOR BOURNE: Better? If you need more water just let us know.

- All right now, sir, just my throat gets a bit dry.

SENATOR BOURNE: You were just explaining how another lifeboat was lowered over the top of lifeboat 13.

- Yes, sir, thank you. Those moments where the lifeboat hovered directly over lifeboat 13 seemed to go on and on. It was such a long way down, nine decks below, too far for anyone to do a thing to help.

But another surge from the waterline shot 13 even further and this time the men rowing followed the direction of it, shooting out from underneath just as the next boat landed on the water. Lifeboat number 13, packed with passengers, rowed into the darkness, leaving the Titanic behind. I noticed only a handful of the sixty-five passengers on board ever looked back.

With my duty done, I noticed that the deck was now at a clear slope. A cup rolled past me down towards the bow and passengers and crew staggered a little.

I looked out to sea. What was out there? Titanic had the Marconi operators and they would call for help. Our route was a common one, there would be ships around us, surely. I decided another ship would come to our rescue. I couldn't imagine the water would engulf the Titanic before we were rescued.

It was about then the calm started to break down. I was dragged into a row of other crew, with an officer barking orders I couldn't make out. Arms linked with mine on either side, forming a chain that blocked a group of third-class male passengers from charging to the last of the lifeboats. They yelled in a variety of languages, but I only recognized the Italian - that was the most common nationality in my section. The men whose cabins I had swept, who often neatly made their beds and wiped their sinks, who were mostly headed to America to start a new life, to find work, to get married, to have families . . .

Instead, now they pressed at my back as I barred their chance of safety, as the deck tilted them closer to the sea. There were no more women and children in my eyeline, I didn't even know why I was blocking them. I think of that a lot now. I stopped them due to orders, but what if I'd known what was going to happen? What if any of us had?

SENATOR BOURNE: You did your duty, Daniels. Disobeying orders would have helped no one.

- Yes, sir. Sorry, sir. Around that time a gunshot rang out. The line broke as the shot stilled the men.

SOLICITOR GENERAL: Who fired the gunshot?

- I didn't see.

SOLICITOR GENERAL: To your knowledge were any of the third-class passengers locked below decks?

- Not to my knowledge, sir.

SENATOR BOURNE: Were passengers being turned away from the final boats?

- Yes, sir. There was this one boy, I judged about my age, who raced to a boat. A woman holding a baby said: 'He's with me - he's my son, he's only twelve, he's tall for his age.'

This boat was packed full with still more women and children being loaded on.

'Would you take the place of a lady or infant, son?' said Officer Moody to the boy.

The boy hung his head. 'No, sir, I would not,' he said.

Then, trying to sound cheerful he called

out, 'There's more boats the other side, Ma, you stop there with Tommy and the baby and I'll see you soon.'

I don't know how that lad walked away so calmly despite the wails of his mother. At that point I thought all the lifeboats from the other side had been launched, and he knew that too.

But not everyone wanted to get on a lifeboat, sir. Many weren't trying to - they were just there on deck, shivering, not knowing what to do.

The slope of the deck was at a mighty tilt. Only an hour or so before, it had been impossible to imagine the ship sinking; now I think we all knew - crew and passengers - that Titanic was going down at the head.

The last lifeboat had an even more frightening journey down the side of the ship, as by then the ship was at such an angle the pulleys weren't working right. The rope on one end of the lifeboat was running, the other was not, and the lifeboat slipped at a steeper slant than the ship. Screams from below, while passengers and sailors in the lifeboat scrabbled at the ropes and clutched each other. Just as it seemed they would all be thrown in, a sailor in a blue engineer's uniform stepped forward. He whacked the jammed davit with a hammer and the pulley ran free, dropping the tipped end of the boat with a huge jerk. It was a miracle no one was tossed out and they clung to each other, terrified. Soon that boat rowed free in the light of two more flares, and their glow gave me a glimpse of all the lifeboats rowing into the distance. Away from the decks still packed with crew and passengers.

It was a blur then, as the ship started sinking more quickly, or that's how I remember it.

The band stopped playing - the slope of the deck must have become too much. I don't know how they continued so long.

A muffled boom from deep in the ship and the slope of the deck increased again. I knew I needed to get to the back of the boat. But what then?

Everyone started moving in the same direction, and I guess they were thinking like I was, hoping to stay on board until the last moment, hoping our flare signals were reaching another ship that would swoop in to rescue us. But if that didn't happen - well, eventually the ship would suck us all down with it. I stopped, hooking my arm around the rail, feet slipping on the tilted deck. If another ship was going to get to us on time, surely we'd see it by now, it was all happening too quickly.

It was only then that I really thought about going into the freezing water.

I checked the straps on my life vest was knotted, remembering how me and the other lads had laughed as we tied them. Where were those boys now?

When the bow of Titanic was swallowed the first real screams came. And they didn't stop.

Another flare lit the boat, now launching from the stern. Another and another. Like a firework display. Panicking groups of passengers skidded and staggered up the deck behind me. An elderly man slipped and fell, knocking other passengers into the water like a bowling ball striking through skittles in Da's pub. There was nothing I could do to help.

Then an almighty creak. One of the magnificent funnels wobbled. I thought it was too big, made of solid steel. I felt like I was seeing things when it crumpled, like a tin can.

2.00 A.M.
FROM: TITANIC
TO: ALL SHIPS

SIGNAL VERY FAINT AND UNREADABLE AS
POWER GREATLY REDUCED

(HEARD BY VIRGINIAN)

UNITED STATES SENATE INQUIRY

Day 10 - 28th April 1912
Testimony of Sidney Daniels

SENATOR BOURNE: At the point the funnel collapsed can you estimate how much of the ship was submerged?

- It's hard to say, sir. Maybe half the deck - yes - the front half was underwater and the slope was too steep to stand on. I felt like I'd have no chance in the icy water, but I had even less chance where I was, gripping to the rails where I would soon only be able to hang on with the strength of my arms. There were explosions, a screeching - the rip of metal I suppose - so loud it hurt my ears and behind it all . . . the screams.

But I did hear a voice cut through the noise saying: 'A knife! Anyone got a knife? Help!'

Lucky for me a single flare went up at that moment, so I saw where the voice was coming from.

A knife. I reached into the top of my life vest with one hand, my whole weight now supported by my elbow hooked around the railing. I scrambled into the breast pocket of my uniform. It had to be there, I always kept it there ever since Da gave it to me.

'I have a knife!' I called into the air,

but my voice was drowned by the racket.

People were now in the waters that covered the deck. Others jumped off the sides and hundreds surged up the sharp slant of the stern deck, trying to hold the railings, to grip anything on board. Many fell and dragged others down with them.

But below me, in the rising water, a group of crew were gathered around something. A piece of canvas. It made no sense at first.

Something was lashed to the roof of the cabins on deck. That was where the call for a knife was coming from.

I realized there was one lifeboat left.

It was different to the other lifeboats, with canvas sides. And it was upside down. The men around it couldn't turn it upright because it seemed to be tethered - as the ship sank further the lifeboat floated, but the Titanic would soon drag it down with it.

I half ran, half slipped across the rising deck, then waded through the icy water to the men, holding up my knife.

That was when I realized how cold the water really was. A vicious stinging cold that snatched at my chest before it reached my waistline.

'Here!' I gasped, and handed the knife to one of the men. His terrified eyes met mine as he snatched it from me, then reached under the water, yelling at his companions. They were all crew.

I knew my only chance was to stay with them.

Then Titanic's lights flashed and went out.

SENATOR BOURNE: Could you tell us what time the power cut off?

- I can't sir. I'm sorry, everything was . . . I don't know.

SENATOR BOURNE: That's quite understandable, Daniels. Please go on, the inquiry will greatly appreciate your full account.

- It went pitch-black then, sir. That was the most frightening part in a way. I can't even remember exactly what I did next, but people all around me screamed and wept. I don't know how I flung myself out of the water and found the ship's rail. That metal pole was almost straight up by then.

My eyes got a little used to the dark, but it really was the darkest night, sir, no moon at all.

I saw the deck would soon be vertical and I was ending up fully in the sea whatever happened. So I climbed the rails.

I balanced on the rim of the deck, rails behind me, the whole ship jerking, explosions rumbling, metal wrenching. And people, so many people, falling, flailing in the water . . .

The boat wasn't only sinking, it was breaking. I know it sounds fanciful, sir, but it sounded like a great iron beast in its dying agony.

SENATOR BOURNE: And whereabouts on the ship were you positioned at this time?

- I was around three-quarters down the deck towards the stern, or around about that, and I was outside the rails but still clinging to them with my arms as I tried not to look down.

Stoker Barratt's words came back to me: 'Stay out of the water, son, and if you can't do that then swim away from the ship fast as you can.'

I forced myself to look down and out at the sea as there were more judders and creaks. The dark water was dotted with white life vests as the boat continued to tip.

I needed to get as far from the hull as possible. It was hovering, trembling, getting ready to plunge.

Up until the very moment I jumped, I really didn't think I could do it.

But I did. I leapt with all of my might, out into the dark.

2. 17 A.M.
FROM: TITANIC
TO: ALL SHIPS

CQ . . .

SIGNAL ENDS ABRUPTLY AS IF POWER
SWITCHED OFF

(HEARD BY VIRGINIAN)

2. 17 A.M.
FROM: VIRGINIAN
TO: TITANIC

TRY EMERGENCY SET

(NO RESPONSE)

UNITED STATES SENATE INQUIRY

SENATOR BOURNE: As you might know by now, Mr Daniels, you were the last of the crew to leave the deck and survive.

- I know, sir, and I am very sorry for it.

SENATOR BOURNE: Please continue - your detailed testimony is extremely valuable to our inquiry.

- So I jumped and next thing I knew the ice water ripped the air from my lungs and froze my legs and arms so I couldn't move. I suppose the life vest saved me then, as I shot up to the surface like a cork, gasping, cold stabbing into every inch of my skin.

I knew I needed to somehow make my body work and swim away from Titanic. Others were around me in the water, jostling me. One man even grabbed me but I shook myself free. All I could see of him were the wide whites of his eyes and his teeth, bared.

Somehow I managed to kick. My legs came back to life.

Maybe the shock of the cold passed for me, but others didn't survive it. Many fell quiet so quickly, limp, held on the surface by their life vests. I didn't think I would get away either but seeing them my legs just kicked and kicked in panic.

I remember I spun around as I swam away from the Titanic and took a glance at the ship.

SENATOR BOURNE: Take your time, Mr Daniels.

- I - I saw the Titanic's stern in the air, gigantic propellers dripping. It was so wrong to see it like that, sir, positioned bow down . . . Like it was diving headfirst, like the whole world turned upside down. People were still on it somehow, falling off the stern.

I swam as fast as I could.

Then I saw the upturned lifeboat I'd helped set free!

The dome of it rose above the water, and men were draped on it, others trying to climb up but slipping back into the sea.

I called out, but couldn't be heard above the cries of the people in the water around me. But the upturned lifeboat was getting nearer, very slowly. They were still dragging people from the water and hadn't yet started rowing.

I glanced back again and caught Titanic's last moment, as the propellers and the final part of the stern disappeared beneath the ocean.

SENATOR BOURNE: What was left behind in the moments after the Titanic disappeared below the surface?

- Just the sea, bubbling like it was boiling. There was debris, deckchairs, broken furniture all around. And many many white life vests.

15th April 1912

2.20 a.m.

(The official time
RMS *Titanic* foundered
at 41.46 N 50.14 W)

UNITED STATES SENATE INQUIRY

SENATOR BOURNE: Welcome back Mr Daniels, I hope your luncheon was suitable? We left off when you were in the sea.

- Yes, sir. Thank you, sir. I thought I had most likely failed to get far enough from the sinking ship and the sea would take me down with it, like Barratt had said. But I swam on, arms cramping in the freezing water, clothes dragging, and no suction came.

I was getting closer to the upside-down collapsible lifeboat again, I could make out individual faces . . . even the man I'd given my knife to.

Then something grasped me - like the sea itself took ahold of me.

SENATOR BOURNE: When you say 'something' you refer to the power of the water?

- Um - I think so, sir.

SENATOR BOURNE: You think so? Surely there was nothing else that could have caused such turbulence?

- That's right, sir. The turbulence of the ship was the only explanation. I was whirled around and expected to be dragged below, but found I remained on the surface. I was in an almighty eddy - a whirlpool of sorts - and it hauled me from the site of the disaster, but also away from that last lifeboat, and into the dark.

No matter how hard I kicked, the current was too strong. Other things were caught in the spiralling water with me, a wooden suitcase, a steamer chair, a lady's straw hat, two life vests without their owners. There was debris too, splintered wood.

When this eddy finally unspooled I drifted in a last spin and blinked into the darkness around me. It was silent.

When I called out, my voice echoed.

I was alone. Half frozen, shivering, teeth chattering, my arms and legs like lead weights, and worst of all I knew there was no hope of a lifeboat now.

I wasn't thinking then, it felt like the end for me, I'd had it good and proper, but somehow I swam to the suitcase. I caught hold of the floating folded wooden steamer chair, somehow shoving the suitcase on to it even though my arms was stiff and clumsy with cold.

I also grabbed the two life vests that had been swept round in the eddy with me. I jammed them either end of the steamer chair through

the slats and the sort of raft floated a
little higher.

SENATOR BOURNE: There must have been plenty
of debris but you are almost the sole
survivor who fashioned a raft in this way.
How did you manage it?

- I can't tell you, sir, I just don't know. I
was lucky with what had been swept up along
with me.

It didn't seem likely I could scramble on
to the contraption I'd put together, but I
slithered and grunted and with enough failed
attempts to almost completely drain the last
of my energy, I finally scrambled on. I
curled up, trying to get as much of me out of
the water as possible, but under my weight
the steamer chair and life vests were almost
submerged and I had to grip the handle of the
suitcase to stop it floating away. My frozen
fingers could barely move.

The wide-brimmed lady's hat I'd seen
floated past and I fished it out and balanced
it atop the suitcase. It stayed there as there
wasn't a breath of wind. Black was all around
me, it felt like more than darkness, like it
were touching me.

A paler shape bobbed past me. At first I
thought it was a life vest. Maybe with a
person . . . I didn't want to, but I reached
out and recoiled. It was hard and smooth.

Sharply cold - my fingers were numb but I felt the bite. Seems strange now, but I didn't realize right away it was ice, not until it was surrounding me.

SENATOR BOURNE: And in all this time did you see any sign of another ship, a flare or hear a horn?

- Nothing, sir.

SENATOR BOURNE: Or any other person? Passenger or crew? Either alive or . . . any remains?

- No, sir. No. I kept crying out for help. My voice was weak from the cold, and I was afraid to tip the raft. I listened for an answer to my calls but it was so quiet. No flares, no lights, no wind.

My eyes got used to the dark and there was stars and in the faint glow of them I made out taller icebergs, smaller lumps and the bunches of icebergs gathered together. I thought that I must be in the middle of what I'd heard called an ice field.

I suppose I'd been hoping I could still be rescued by ships but they weren't going to come in among all this ice.

I can't describe how cold I was, my wet clothes hardening into ice against my body, leaching the last warmth out of me. It was

like the stiffness of my frozen clothing held
my body in place.

It was only then I noticed the monogram on
the suitcase beneath me.

J.T.G.

I wondered if it had belonged to a man or a
lady . . . and hoped they made it to a lifeboat.
Before then I'd just thought of the suitcase
as something that floated, not as a suitcase
of clothes. Dry clothes. I imagined how it
would feel to be dry, warm, just once more.

When I raised myself on to my elbows from
my curled position, the steamer chair tipped
so my feet were in the water. I wouldn't be
able to move let alone change clothes without
pitching into the icy water. I thought the
inside of the case was probably soaked
through anyway. But then a huge flat iceberg
drifted towards me. It was almost like a
piece of land, a white island.

SENATOR BOURNE: Were you not terribly stiff
by now, son?

- Yes, sir, I really was. I circled my shoulders and flexed my elbows and wrists
carefully without rocking the raft too much
as I watched the iceberg drift slowly towards
me. When it came within reach I grabbed the
suitcase and swung it on to the berg as it
passed. I was sunk in the water without the
suitcase keeping me afloat and I spluttered,

grasping at the steamer chair and life vests, thinking I wouldn't surface again, but I did. I saw the case spinning across the icy island. I expected it to skid right across until it slid off the other side and was lost.

But it slowed and stopped and there was no going back now. If there were dry clothes in that case, they were my only chance.

I think I just sort of stumbled and lunged, and tried to jump as the lower part of the iceberg passed me. I almost didn't make it. I landed on my belly, then was pulled slithering backwards, grasping at the ice with my fingernails. It wasn't an upwards slope, if anything the edge of the iceberg was higher - so why . . .

I realized my foot was caught in the ties of one of the life vests. I kicked as hard as I could to free myself from the raft that had saved me but now threatened to kill me after all.

Suddenly my legs were free, or at least almost free and I hauled myself up, fingers finding a tiny crack in the ice. Panting and hiccupping on the ice, I saw one of the life vests was still attached to my leg by its tie. I hauled it up on to the iceberg with me.

SENATOR BOURNE: How were you not slipping and sliding on this ice?

- I was, sir. But although it was ice, it wasn't completely smooth, more like when the ice on an ice rink has been messed up by hundreds of skaters. Lumpy ice, like a broken edge of a rock.

SENATOR BOURNE: Thank you for explaining, do continue.

- Well, the life vest that almost killed me might have also been what saved my life. The first thing I did when I stopped shaking and panting and retrieved the suitcase was to sit on the life vest to stop the cold passing right through my clothes. It was here that I worked on the lock of the case. I patted my breast pocket, then remembered I had given the knife to the sailor to free the collapsible lifeboat.

I searched my other pockets, shocked how numb my hands were - I couldn't feel whether there was anything in them or not at first. Then I located my keys on the chain around my neck.

They would have to do. I stabbed at the wood of the case, and my arms warmed up a little and started tingling, I don't mind saying that it hurt mightily. And the life vest I was sitting on along with the case itself was both skidding around on the iceberg.

SENATOR BOURNE: Did the iceberg rock at all?

- No, sir. I didn't wonder about that at the time, but I think it must have had a very great load of ice underwater to hold it steady. Of course I know a bit more about icebergs now.

When I finally broke through the wood, the case sprung open.

I stared inside. For a start it was dry. It had belonged to a man and looked like a first-class passenger's at that. Fine woollen suits, smooth shirts, a paisley silk scarf . . . I pulled out a jacket. It was huge across the middle but strangely short.

What with me a tall skinny lad, it wasn't perfect but it felt perfect to me.

I ruffled through the clothes, and holding the dry cloth up to my face made me feel warmer already. I was almost overcome with my luck, but knew I'd need as many layers as possible if I was ever to have any chance of getting warm, and I didn't fancy my chances even then.

So I - well, sir, I put them on.

SENATOR BOURNE: You got changed? On the iceberg?

- I did, sir. I tackled my bottom half first. My hard frozen wet slacks seemed to be stuck fast, but finally I peeled them off only to find, of course, they was stuck to my boots.

And there I was, glancing all around to

check I wasn't exposing myself even though I'd be so delighted to see another person if there was one, well - I wouldn't care if my drawers were out or not!

Sorry, sir. I never thought how funny it must have looked till I was telling . . . you . . .

SENATOR BOURNE: When you have composed yourself, please do continue, Mr Daniels.

- Yes, sir, sorry, sir. I pulled on one pair of long johns, and my legs was so cold it was like they was sticky and it was a mighty struggle but easier after that, and I was warming up, tingling. I added two pairs of silk pyjama bottoms, tightened by their cords, then a pair of the thickest wool trousers. I fumbled with the suspenders so they would stay up; some of my fingers were still frozen, the others tingling. The layers bulked me up but the relief was quicker than I thought, my thighs prickling painfully as I sat back on the life vest to peel off my boots and socks. I hauled on some silky white dress socks, two pairs, followed by some thick woollen ones. I couldn't feel my toes.

The brown brogue boots I found were strangely about the right size with the layers of socks. The fine leather gleamed softly in the starlight. I stood and immediately skidded as I'd made a smooth patch of ice where I was standing and it was very slippery now. I looked at my own sodden boots, rimmed with frost, then back at the suitcase. There was another pair of chunky woollen socks in a darker colour, although I couldn't see what colour in the dark. I hauled the coarse wool on over the boots and tested them on the ice.

SENATOR BOURNE: So despite having been fully submerged in the water, you had the good fortune and sense to strip off your wet and frozen garments? How did you know to do that?

- I didn't, sir. Just the cold hurt, I would do anything to stop it.

I wasn't keen to strip my top half but the way my legs were warming, tingling and painful, I knew I had no choice. A few minutes later I was wrapped in dry vests, two silk pyjama tops, two shirts, two fine woollen waistcoats and two jackets. I wrapped the scarf around my neck and tucked it in. No hat. No gloves. I looked at what was left. The other pair of suit trousers and a third pair of woollen socks. Whoever the case belonged to seemed to really like having warm feet, and wasn't I glad for it! I put the waist of the spare trousers over my head, then wrapped the legs around to tie it in a kind of headdress instead of a hat.

With the socks pulled over my hands only my face was left uncovered.

2.28 A.M. *
FROM: LA PROVENCE
TO: CELTIC

NOBODY HAS HEARD TITANIC FOR ABOUT
2 HOURS

* All times from here on are New York time: one hour
fifty minutes behind *Titanic* time

When the *Carpathia* finally makes it out from among the icebergs, the sky is turning deep blue with dawn. We have been travelling for hours, but the time went quickly, and now I stand between Rigel and Captain Rostron at the bow. There's a jagged white horizon to the left of the ship that the captain says is the ice field.

Rigel quietly pants beside me, no longer signalling the presence of something beneath the water only he can tell is there: the sea serpent circling the icebergs, making waves break against their base, allowing the captain to navigate. I am sure the creature got us through the ice-bergs safely – but not deliberately. What does it want? I shiver at the thought.

An officer passes a note to Captain Rostron. 'We are close to where the last *Titanic* message was sent, sir, coordinates are here.'

I suddenly need to see my cousin.

Harry's hair stands on end and there is a stale smell in the Marconi room but still I shut the door behind me to keep out the cold as my cousin is in his shirtsleeves. I guess he hasn't been to bed.

'Harry? Are you all right?' I say, wishing now I'd got a mug of tea or something for him. He spins around; his eyes are bright against dark circles and his skin has a sickly sheen to it. My heart seems to still when I meet his eyes.

'Clara.' He forces a smile.

'What's happening – have any ships seen *Titanic*?'

I see his throat move as if swallowing something too large. 'I don't know if they are going to find her, Clara, no other ships have heard anything.

'The captain sent a message to tell *Titanic* all our boats were ready and we were coming as fast as we could, with a double watch on in the engine room, and to be prepared, when we got there, with lifeboats. I hope they heard me, Clara. Because I got no acknowledgement of that message, or any I sent after.'

'Maybe their Marconi machine got broken?'

'I hope so. What we do know is they said they were putting passengers in lifeboats hours ago. It's freezing out there.'

Where I thought Harry's eyes were bright, now I see that it's more like with Folly, when she's got the wind up her tail and can't stop running even though she's tired out.

The horn sounds again.

'Could that mean they've found something?' I say to Harry.

'It could. I need to stay here but you should go see. But keep the dog out of the way, Clara, please. The captain has taken a liking to you, but he needs to concentrate – whatever happens next.'

My mouth drops open at the unfairness of that, but he's already turned round.

'I was with the captain, Harry, in the icebergs, and Rigel helped . . .' I say, then trail off at the expression on his face. More than anything I want Harry to respect me.

'Just make sure you don't cause any trouble, Clarty. No antics. This is serious.'

Rigel whines and licks my hand as I'm dismayed to find myself blinking back hot tears. I take a deep cold breath of the air on deck.

Crew are gathered at the bow of the ship and I rush to join a crowd of passengers, and Bernie snapping away with her camera.

'We just passed a huge berg. I caught it, I think there's just enough light. Could be the one that hit the *Titanic*.'

'What's happening?' I say. 'Why are the horns sounding?'

'No one seems to know,' she says, 'but they say there's been a light spotted – a green light.'

'From *Titanic*?'

'That's what I heard,' she says.

Rigel licks my hand and sits. I bury my gloved hand in the fur behind his ears, then stare out to sea in the direction that everyone else is staring.

A yelp from Bernie. Others pointing. Rigel stands, tail wagging, and then I see it. A white lifeboat rowing towards us. Other dots in the distance.

'If passengers are in lifeboats, has the *Titanic* gone … down?' I say.

People mutter and turn and glare at me. No one answers.

'She's only saying what you're all thinking,' says Bernie.

3. 15 A. M.
FROM: CARPATHIA
TO: TITANIC

IF YOU ARE THERE WE ARE FIRING
ROCKETS

UNITED STATES SENATE INQUIRY

SENATOR BOURNE: Can you tell us a little more about the iceberg you were on?

- Once I was all trussed up in the clothing from the suitcase, I could look around. The ice-berg seemed around the size of the third-class saloon on the Titanic which seated two hundred people. The flat part of the ice was only around half of the total area, the rest rose in a peak.

When I looked over the edge - in one area I could just make out a shadow below. It was so dark, sir, but I could just see what I thought was a reflection of the ice above it . . . and I realized it was the base of the iceberg.

I'd been trying not to think of Titanic, the sound the iceberg had made as we slept in the third-class stewards' berth. But then I imagined the iceberg tearing a hole way below the waterline, because we didn't see any damage up on deck.

When I saw the ghostly underwater shape of the berg I realized the sky was changing. No longer inky - its deep blue was washed out towards the horizon.

I was so relieved to see dawn. With the

sunrise I could tell which direction I was facing at least, not that it would be any help to me. I tried to remember the direction the Titanic was travelling - west to America. And the lifeboats had rowed away from her so had they been heading west? If there was any possibility of help coming, would it come from the west towards New York?

My excitement at the return of the light was soon replaced by a fear just as strong. Because as the sky lightened, I saw the ice field had no end. The light became red and orange and tinted the ice around me so it reminded me of tinned peaches bobbing, and the sea so flat it could have been the syrup.

But my spirits dipped, because there was no sign of another soul.

Already my mouth was parched. By getting myself warm I'd simply chosen one death over the other. I started to suspect it would be more painful to thirst to death than it would have been to freeze.

At first I paced up and down the iceberg, I don't know how long for. But I got so tired, and the ice became more slippery where I'd been walking on it, the socks over my shoes now frozen solid. Where would I be if I slipped and broke a bone? Wishing I'd frozen in the water in the first place. But when I imagined the icy sting of the sea, attacking my skin again, that horrible ache, I was grateful to be out of it despite how bleak my future looked.

I opened out the life vest so it was one long piece, closed the suitcase and put it at the end so I had a makeshift bed.

I burrowed my now warmed fingers deeper into my armpits as I lay down. I curled on my side and watched the sky colour change to pink then blue, and tried not to think at all.

15ᵗʰ

April

1912

4.10 a.m.

(At approximately daybreak the first
lifeboat is brought aboard *Carpathia*)

33

The first lifeboat pulls alongside the *Carpathia* and I lean over the rails, taken aback by the expressionless faces of the *Titanic* passengers. I can't see injuries, and they seem mostly to be bundled in hats and coats. These people are fine, they aren't crying, they don't even seem hurt, just cold. Maybe the *Titanic* didn't sink after all – it could be just over the horizon. I hug Rigel close, hoping.

The crew encourage the *Titanic* passengers up rope ladders; all is quiet, organized and very very strange. Rigel leans his shoulder at my hip, and I can tell he is wagging hard. Bernie's camera clicks away. Then my eyes focus on a woman's hand, gloveless, shaking. She reaches for a rung of the rope ladder but her hand slips and she falls back into the boat, caught by a sailor with the White Star sign on his cap. At first I think her hands must simply be too cold, and that even I wouldn't be silly enough to go without gloves in this temperature. But when she falls to her knees I see she is wearing a long nightgown and satin slippers beneath her coat. Her head shakes, and she points back in the direction she came, clasping both hands in front of her, as if praying.

I feel sick. Bernie turns to look at me and her face is grim.

An officer calls down, 'News of the *Titanic*?'

The sailors who were rowing the boat glance at each other, their faces flushed with the effort but with the same grim haunted look as the passengers.

'She foundered, sir, and many souls with her,' one says in a trembling voice and crosses himself as if in church.

Foundered? What does it mean?

A soft gasp rises from both the passengers in the lifeboat and those who wait to bring them on board.

The word seems to spread and echo across the frozen sea.

One woman cries out and crumples over in the bottom of the lifeboat.

I think I can guess now, but I don't want to be right. I nudge Bernie. 'Foundered?' I whisper.

She takes a deep breath and doesn't look up from her camera as she mutters, 'Lost. It means sunk.'

The other women on board the lifeboat – it seems that this boat is almost all women – talk to the one who collapsed and she wipes her face with the heel of her hand and finally climbs the rope ladder. I can't see what happens at the top, but I presume she is swept away by the *Carpathia* passengers who are holding steamer blankets and even comforters from their beds, ready to wrap up the frozen *Titanic* passengers as they come aboard.

The expression on that woman's face, hours in the cold and dark, maybe split up from loved ones. This is the most dreadful situation I've ever seen anyone in.

A large sack is hauled up the side of the boat and I remember the captain's words. 'Canvas bags – for the children.'

I shudder and swallow hard. There has to be some way I can help.

Everyone is busy, all seeming to know what they are supposed to be doing, and Harry's words still ring painfully in my chest, as I worry I will only be in the way. I stay close to Bernie even though when she notices, she gives me a glare and widens the space between us. She's probably worried Rigel will jog her precious camera again, although he's silent, close by my side.

The passengers are brought aboard more quickly now, and either bundled off to form orderly lines at the tea and coffee urns or helped below deck or into the first-class saloon. I count the boats: five of them have now unloaded their dejected passengers. What would it be like to see a steamship sink? And your loved ones with it? Beyond imagining. That's why they are mostly quiet, pale, rather – they are shocked and frozen.

Rigel tugs gently at the leash and I follow him to where two very small children sit on a steamer chair, bundled together in a blanket. A nurse crouches to the side, talking to them in a soft voice, and I hear her ask their names but both stare straight ahead as if they haven't heard. I remember how Rigel was with Yolanda, the girl with the toys, and her brother, John.

'Good, Rigel,' I whisper, 'have you found someone who might need you?'

The small boys continue to stare at nothing. I wonder if they are badly injured.

I lead Rigel up to the children. He looks back at me and I nod. He noses the boy's chest. The boy's head wobbles on his neck as if he is a doll, not a child at all. To my surprise, the nurse with them doesn't stop the dog.

'This is Rigel. He likes children and he is really gentle.' I drop my voice. 'What's wrong with them?'

An officer spins around. 'Get that animal off deck immediately, this is not—'

'Leave the dog be,' snaps the nurse. 'These children are half-catatonic, in grave danger from shock and cold. Dogs similar to this are used in mountain rescue.'

The larger of the two boys reaches out a small bluish hand to Rigel and the dog licks it then nuzzles his neck. The kid buries both his hands in the fuzz below Rigel's ears. Then this boy takes his little brother's hand and holds it out to the dog. Rigel dutifully licks it and when the younger boy spreads his arms, Rigel bounces both front legs on to the armrests and the two boys hold the huge dog around the neck, their tiny arms buried in his thick black fur. The smaller boy's hands are chubby like a starfish; he's barely more than a baby. He releases a gurgling giggle when Rigel licks his nose.

The officer tenses but doesn't interfere.

'Papa?' says the oldest boy.

'*Quel est ton nom?*' says the nurse. The boys must be French.

Nothing – they concentrate on Rigel.

'They haven't spoken until now, so we haven't been able to examine either of them, and they may be injured,' whispers the nurse.

'*Je suis Michel et mon frère est Edmond*,' says the oldest boy.

I lead Rigel away from the boys, who now move and take the nurse's hand, allowing themselves to be led inside, into the warm. 'Good boy, Rigel. Very good boy.'

I scan across the deck and see an elderly lady in a steamer chair, her eyes shut, face grey. When she sees Rigel she smiles and pets him and Rigel puts his chin up for her to scratch.

'Oh, you like that, don't you?' she says in a wobbly voice. She smiles but I'm taken aback by her eyes. She looks . . . haunted. Terrified. I take her hand between both of mine and it's so cold. I have no idea what to say to her.

'Could you look after Rigel while I fetch you some tea?' I say. I raise a hand to show Rigel to wait. I pop behind the urn and fetch hot tea for the lady. When I get back she has a patch of colour in each cheek. I see a boy on his own, standing at the rails looking out. He is wearing blue check pyjamas, an overcoat and a baker's boy hat. I tap him on the arm and when he turns I see he's only about my age.

'My brothers and father. They—'

He doesn't finish. He drops to a crouch in front of Rigel and buries his face in the dog's fur, his shoulders shuddering.

6. 45 A.M.
FROM: CARPATHIA
TO: MOUNT TEMPLE

WE ARE NOW RESCUING TITANIC'S
PASSENGERS

As the surviving *Titanic* passengers pile on to the *Carpathia*, Rigel seems to sense who will get some comfort from him, and guides me, sitting quietly by people of all ages while I fetch their hot drinks. Although the deck of the *Carpathia* is busy, I expect the stream of lifeboats to continue for the rest of the day as the *Titanic* was such a huge liner, and the lifeboats seem small.

Some of the rescued gather along the rail staring out at the horizon waiting to see who is on the next lifeboat each time one comes closer, desperate to find their husbands, sons. Most of the passengers who have come aboard are ladies and children.

It isn't long before there are no more lifeboats on the horizon. But that doesn't seem right. There are too few people for a boat like *Titanic*, far too few, even I can see that.

The atmosphere is calm, ordered, quiet. The weather is the same, sun now well above the horizon, a clear day again, and its bright glare makes what has happened here seem all the more impossible.

Foundered. I've only ever thought of a shipwreck as something that happens in a storm. This sea is like glass. One large iceberg has broken free of the ice field and looms to the left, glistening palest blue.

Carpathia glides slowly and there are shards of wood in the water, a child's toy, life jackets. I don't want to look too closely and instead follow the path of what might be the final lifeboat as it slowly draws nearer to us.

Carpathia stops. This lifeboat only contains half as many people as the others. An older lady and a man row, and as they draw closer I see the man has soot on his face. They approach slowly.

So does the iceberg.

An officer calls something down to the sailor.

That iceberg is getting too close.

'Hold hard to port,' he yells, and I'm not sure what

happens next but somehow the lifeboat is caught in a churn of water from the turning ship, and is dragged towards the front, round the bow and out of sight. I grip the rails; that iceberg is too close, it seems the lifeboat will be crushed between it and the *Carpathia* . . .

Voices call out, but I am distracted.

'Rigel!'

The huge dog's front paws are up on the top rail, his tail between his legs, ears up.

'Down, boy.' I try to grasp his rope, rushing towards him. He's been so good with all the survivors, I haven't been holding his leash. His back legs spring on to the second of the rails, slip, then gain grip. I've seen him do this before.

'No, Rigel!'

I lunge at him, but the dog springs from the side of the ship and I am left only with the softest touch of his fur as I watch him sail through the air and splash into the sea below.

8.00 A.M.
FROM: CARPATHIA
TO: VIRGINIAN

TELL YOUR SKIPPER WE ARE LEAVING
HERE WITH ALL ON BOARD. ABOUT 800
PASSENGERS. PLEASE RETURN TO YOUR
NORTHERN COURSE.

35

The moments when Rigel disappears underwater are the longest in my life. How could I have let this happen twice? I should have been taking better care of him!

Then a slick black head pops out of the water.

Everyone on deck gathers along the rail.

'Rigel!' I yell. He turns, looks up, once, right at me, then swims determinedly on, surprisingly fast in the water. When he jumped for the children's toy he was bobbing in the ship's churning wake, but in the calm sea, with his fur slicked down, he's like a different animal completely, one made for the sea, strong front legs swooping by the sides of his body as he swims.

I run alongside the rail, barging other passengers out of the way. 'Rigel, Rigel!'

The only thing on my mind is that I can't let that black head out of my sight. I keep up with him as he paddles to the front of the ship. The large iceberg passes us safely by with gasps from the passengers but my eyes cling only to Rigel. The lifeboat that was around the front of the ship comes into sight.

One of the lifeboat passengers waves their hand as if batting away a giant fly.

It's only then I realize that the dog has jumped in because he heard the cries of distress, and he's trying to help.

I push through as close to the lifeboat as I can and call down. The lifeboat is now back by the rope ladders and passengers are quickly being helped out. These people have spent more time in the small boat than anyone and look half frozen.

'The dog is just trying to help, he's friendly,' I call down to them.

'Call him off immediately,' floats up a man's pompous-sounding voice.

I remember what the nurse said. 'He's a rescue dog, he's trying to help you!' I yell. People around me tut, no doubt thinking I'm an incredibly rude child. But right now I care less than I ever have.

Then the man, who seems to be wearing evening dress, grabs hold of one of the oars and starts to slap at Rigel's head, forcing the dog to duck under, out of the way.

I scream, 'No – don't hurt him!' and climb on to the first rung of the railing, better to shout down. I feel arms holding me back.

I blink away furious tears to see Rigel has swum well out of the way of the stupid man and some of the women in the boat have wrestled the oar off him. A clear voice rings out.

'Eh, give over, mister, you'll have us all in the drink!'

The grip holding me loosens and a voice I recognize calms me. 'What is going on here?'

Captain Rostron is by my side, the other passengers clearing back as the crew efficiently unload the last lifeboat.

I turn to the captain and can't help myself. I grab his arm, I'm so relieved to see him.

'Oh, sir, Rigel jumped in, right off the rails, to go and help when the lifeboat went round the front of the ship, but they were trying to hit him, to beat him with an oar!'

I'm beseeching the captain with my eyes but he doesn't look at me, instead staring out to sea with a slight frown.

I turn. I've only taken my eyes off Rigel for a moment but now I see what the captain is looking at.

Rigel is swimming away from the ship, towards the ice field.

I call again and again but he's so fast and already so far away. Where is that darn dog going now?

'Please, Rigel! It's all right, Rigel, come!'

At my final screech, Rigel turns. He barks once and his black tail lifts out of the water like a flag. Even at the rapidly increasing distance, this doesn't look like a dog swimming for his life. I clap my hands and other passengers do the same.

'Yes, Rigel, come back,' I call, my voice now hoarse from shouting. The black head changes direction, facing me, and I call out again. But Rigel's path makes a loop. He barks again, circles twice and each time I know he is looking right at me, trying to tell me something.

Every time this dog has tried to tell me something before, he's been right. He can feel when the sea serpent is near. But if that's what he's trying to tell me now, what in blazes is he doing in the water with it?

Rigel speeds off towards the ice field, leaving a slim line of wake behind him. He grows smaller as my calls become more cracked, and the claps of the passengers die away.

36

'm frantic, shaking the captain's arm.

'We need to go after him!' I yell. 'Turn the boat, go get him!'

Boiling tears spill from my eyes. Rigel is now winding between the flat icebergs Harry called growlers. Like the one Rigel helped us dodge just the night before. Then I gasp. He is trying to climb up on one. It's too small and tips him back in.

I moan. He's gone too far, he's too cold and now we are going to watch him drown – or is he trying to keep out of the water, to escape something beneath that is tracking him? I can see that snaggled jaw in my mind . . .

But finally, Rigel manages to scrabble on to the ice. He shakes and I can't help but smile through the tears that are now freezing on my cheeks, because at least he's out of the water.

Rigel lifts his head to the sky and there is too much noise on deck, everyone watching the huge black dog, but I'm sure I catch that single determined bark. His tail whips back and forth, a silhouette against the icebergs gathered behind him.

'He's waiting for me,' I whisper. I wipe my eyes and running nose on my gloves and take a huge freezing breath. The pain in my chest brings me out of my panic. I release the captain's arm, refusing to be embarrassed at my outburst and swipe at my face with my mittens.

'You know he's special, you know he can sense things,' I say to the captain, making my voice calm now, not allowing my eyes to leave the tiny toy figure of my dog.

'Help me go to him, please, sir.'

Silence. Others are gathered around me and the captain. I hear the click of Bernie's camera and grimace. Then her voice. 'What if the dog has found another survivor out there? The girl is right about dogs rescuing people. Haven't you heard of those big St Bernards that carry brandy round their neck for that reason?'

Doesn't matter if she is trying to help me and Rigel, or

she's just trying to get more photos, I want to hug Bernie Palmer that minute.

The captain doesn't answer, but he beckons over one of the officers who is standing nearby after bringing the last of the passengers on the lifeboat aboard.

Of all people it is Third Officer Greeve.

'Prepare the tender,' says the captain quietly. 'We'll manoeuvre *Carpathia* a little closer, then you can row out to the animal. We need to check the edge of the ice field to ensure no survivors have been missed.'

The officer opens his mouth as if to argue. I do the same. Of all the officers the captain could choose, did it really have to be this one?

'Is there a question about my order, Greeve? You are ex-Navy, and from a fishing family, which made me think you were the man for the job,' says the captain. 'Was I mistaken? As an envoy of the *Carpathia* we need an officer. You will take Miss Scott with you, to handle the dog.'

This time I slam my mouth closed. If Captain Rostron is getting me to my dog, I'll go with the devil himself.

Rigel is on the iceberg, tail in that determined wag. Waiting for me, trusting I'll come.

I'll find out what he's trying to tell me.

I'm coming, boy.

The captain sends a messenger to fetch my cousin Harry. Rigel is still on that same piece of ice. Is the sea serpent out there too?

'It seems we are in a bit of a quandary, Mr Cottam,' the captain says when Harry races up to us. 'As Miss Scott's only relative on board I will need your permission for something quite irregular.'

Harry seems even more tired than he did before. The captain looks at me, I look at Harry, then back out at the tiny silhouette of Rigel, now growing gradually larger as the steamer moves towards him.

Wait there, boy, just wait.

'Please, Harry – say yes. I need to go to Rigel, he's trying to show me something, I know he is!'

Harry's serious frown reminds me of Pa; some faces are naturally cheerful and a serious expression is just wrong on them. My gut churns with sudden homesickness. As the captain explains that Officer Greeve will row us out to Rigel, Harry shakes his head. It is only when the captain mentions he is fearful there are more survivors, that they don't know if all the lifeboats have been accounted for and that Rigel seems to have some expertise in sea rescue, that my cousin hangs his head as if defeated.

'My young cousin is now this dog's . . . handler?' says Harry.

'It seems so, Cottam,' says Captain Rostron. 'I can't say it's an ideal situation, but it is where we are.'

'Well, I don't think I'm qualified to say no or yes, sir. I daresay my aunt or uncle wouldn't dream of giving permission in ordinary times . . .' He bites his lip. 'But these are not ordinary times.' Harry takes me by surprise, dragging me into a tight hug. 'You listen to the officer, Clara, you hear me. This is serious. Dangerous.'

I wait for him to say something else, about not messing about, about *antics*, but he doesn't and that's somehow worse. I nod into his chest, and when I look up his expression is so serious it pinches my heart. Because he doesn't even know how dangerous it might be. The captain is letting me go . . . but the captain has never seen the sea serpent properly, not like I have.

Rigel wouldn't call me to him if it were dangerous, would he?

'Thank you, Harry. No antics, I promise.'

He shoots me a watery smile and I'm whisked off to find suitable clothing to take a boat trip, my eyes dragging back to Rigel, on that iceberg, waiting for me.

Third Officer Greeve glowers and tuts beneath the rim of his cap as he rows us away from the *Carpathia* towards Rigel. I don't care, and I don't take my eyes off the dog. The wind blowing in my face stings my cheeks but the sea remains entirely flat. The captain insisted on me wearing thick oilskin overalls – the smallest ones he could find from the crew needed knots tied in the braces – a sou'wester hat and a pair of gumboots that my feet are swimming in.

I turn and see Harry watching from the deck rails, even though he should probably be back at his post in the Marconi room.

Once in the rowing boat, which the officers call a tender, Greeve makes long impatient strokes of the oars and we gain on Rigel.

The sea around us is a foreboding deep grey and flat calm – and I try not to imagine a long shadow below us.

I hope Rigel was just spooked by that man whacking at him with the oar. But this dog isn't a skittish foal. As we draw nearer, I call out to him, but he paces on the ice, tail high, barking sharply. Seems he's going to force us to come to him. The officer curses beneath his breath.

His rowing slows as we cruise towards the small iceberg where Rigel stands, like the king of a new land, releasing sharp high barks like orders. My heart swells – we are so close, the thought of reaching him chases away my fears about what else is out here.

'You need to get that hound on board, missy, quick smart,' says Greeve. As we row around Rigel's iceberg the dog continues to bark then raises his nose and sniffs out towards the ice field.

'Stay Rigel, stay!' I yell.

But the dog does the opposite: he leaps into the sea and swims off into the ice field, his slick black head zigzagging between small bergs and growlers.

The wind chooses that moment to pick up and the rowing boat, along with the ice around us, begins to shudder and rock.

Rigel turns to stare at me as he swims, upright tail like a flag.

'That's it,' says Officer Greeve. 'The animal's gone mad. I mean madder than it was to begin with. We can't go any further.'

38

'We can't leave him!' I don't mean to shout but can't help it.

Rigel clambers on to another iceberg in the distance, shakes and turns again, barking. Waiting for me.

'I was given orders to check for anything from the *Titanic*, survivors or another lifeboat,' says Greeve through gritted teeth. 'Can you see anything like that?'

Greeve won't go to him. Nobody cares about a dog, left in a will to a stranger.

Except me. I care.

The officer grasps the oars and starts to row with one

of them, dipping the other deep into the water, turning the boat. I can't let him do this. I climb over the bench in the boat and grasp the other oar tight with both hands.

'Now see here, missy, release that oar at once.'

I hold the oar tight with both hands as he tries to wrench it from my grip. 'No! The captain said you should go to Rigel.'

'The captain isn't here now, child, and I am the ranking officer on this boat!'

'You are disobeying orders!' I scream.

Third Officer Greeve stands in the boat, releasing his hold on the other oar so he can try to wrestle this one off me. The boat sways from side to side, water slopping. The officer's face is turning purple, his eyes disappearing beneath an outraged scowl. He's leaning back, so much stronger than me, I can't hold it—

'My father said you are an unmanageable and impertinent child. The captain should have locked you back in the hold with that mutt. It's been nothing but a—'

I don't know if he is going to say *antics* because I don't give him a chance to finish.

I let go just at the right – or wrong – moment.

It's like at the farm when we used to play tug of war, and my brothers were stronger but we girls would always catch them out, waiting until they were pulling their hardest, really leaning into it, then letting go. They'd go flying. It was a dirty trick, but it was never a fair fight in the first place.

Third Officer Greeve flies backwards, just like the boys did. He reaches behind to stop himself, but his hand slips, his head meets the bench, and there's a sickening crack.

The ship's officer yowls in pain and lies upside down in the bottom of the boat like an upended turtle. There's a bleeding gash on his head and he draws shuddering breaths, cradling one arm with the other.

'You broke my ruddy arm!'

Horsefeathers.

39

Third Officer Greeve is in such pain he allows me to help get him up from the bottom of the rocking boat and on to the bench. I'm taken aback by his grimace and yelps of pain.

'I'm sorry, I didn't mean . . .' I say, unable to find a handkerchief in the borrowed oilskin, so the blood drips down the side of his face.

I watch in horror as he rolls up his sleeve. His wrist looks awful, a huge lump pressing at the skin, and a pooling black bruise around it. He needs to see a doctor.

We have to get back to the *Carpathia*, now.

'Rigel!' I yell. 'I need you!' The dog is on another iceberg, not even that far away. I see the glint of his eyes but his barks are snatched by the wind. He's not going to come to me.

The wind is now gusting, and the floating ice thumps against our boat. The *Carpathia* is nowhere in sight, any view we might have had blocked by icebergs big and small, crowding around us.

This is bad, real bad.

'Officer Greeve, I need you to show me how to row and which way,' I say in my strictest voice.

His face is greyish and he draws a shuddering breath as he stares about him. When his eyes widen in alarm, my heart shrinks. The ice is shifting us in circles, penning us in.

He points away from Rigel. 'Is it that way?' he says.

He's asking *me*?

'Do you have a compass?' I say. 'Don't all officers carry a compass?'

The pain on his face turns to anger. He bites his lip, shaking his head.

'What about an eyeglass?'

'For pity's sake, of course I don't have a compass or an eyeglass. I wasn't expecting to be in the middle of an ice field, was I?'

I want to retort, but don't think it's very good for a

badly injured man to get more riled up. Both of us scan around us. Everything looks the same.

Except in one direction there is a big black dog on an iceberg, barking.

'Shut that animal up!' yells Third Officer Greeve.

No. That's it. Rigel can sense things that no one else can see, so he can sense the way back to the *Carpathia*, I know he can. Third Officer Greeve is no use to me whatsoever in his state. I'm on my own, and I'll make the decisions.

'The dog can help,' I say.

'Help? The blasted dog got us in this mess,' says Greeve.

We fall silent, staring at each other, until finally the man shakes his head.

Third Officer Greeve shows me how to row without complaint; all his energy seems taken up by the pain. I have to help him and this is the only way.

The oars pull hard on my shoulders but I don't mind that. I've always been strong for my age, never letting anyone help me lift heavy things, shifting hay bales with the rest of the family as a matter of pride, and I'm sure glad of it now. But this takes more than strength – I need both arms to work at the same time. I progress slowly, keep the movement smooth, and the tender shoots forward, cutting a path through the ice-scattered water.

Again, again, then the oar sticks like it's in treacle and I have to drop the other to grab it with both hands.

I row some more, this time not going deep enough and skimming the surface, almost hitting myself in the face as the handle of the oar pivots back at me.

Rigel barks, tail wagging. My dog believes in me. I need to keep going.

The new wind picks up white tops from the waves between the ice and throws them at me as I row towards Rigel. I get stronger and faster despite my aching arms. Rigel grows closer.

Small pieces of ice knock against the boat and taller icebergs loom in front of me. Could our boat be crushed between them?

I don't stop rowing.

Sweat drips down my back through the layers and my face is hot despite the chill of the wind. I can barely see as the brim of the sou'wester hat is tipped forward against the wind so it won't blow off. But I am gaining on Rigel, the dog remains balanced on a small iceberg, and this time he's not moving.

'Rigel – please, please just come here,' I plead, then yell with the last of my voice. 'Rigel, I need you to get us home!' This time I feel tearful for real.

There is a large, pointed iceberg to my right and I use only my left oar to steer away from it. I'm right in the ice field now, growlers and icebergs on every side.

Rigel barks. Wags.

I draw in a breath so sharp it hurts my chest.

As I pull closer to the dog he barks at a pointed iceberg, towering. It sails slowly past me, must be catching the wind. On the other side it is flatter and raised above the water, and just below my eyeline is ... a bundle.

Something dark, something red.

Something that definitely doesn't belong there.

'Officer Greeve – look,' I say.

The man's face is too pale. He blinks and shakes his head in disbelief. He looks as if he is on the verge of fainting.

Rigel swims to the iceberg with the bundle, but it is just too far from the sea level for him to jump up.

'Up, Rigel! Come. Get up!'

He needs to get into the tender with me, then he can jump on the side of the boat and on to the iceberg. I don't want to climb out and see what he's found first.

Finally the dog seems to listen to me. Rigel scrambles up the side of the boat and I shift my weight to the opposite side but it tips so steeply I think for a moment that we're going to be swamped. Officer Greeve groans.

But then it pings upright and Rigel is here.

Rigel is here.

I grab my soaked friend, not caring about the wet as I

hug him tight. He stinks of wet dog and the sea but I don't care. I hold his cheeks and let him lick my face all over with that big hot tongue.

After a couple of moments I can't stop him springing out of my arms and up on to the iceberg. I kneel up on the bench of the boat and I see. The shape is a bundled person.

Please, please, please.

This person – this person must be a survivor of the *Titanic*.

Please don't let us be too late.

40

Rigel bounds up to the person huddled on the iceberg. When he bends his head forward, I know by the way his tail wags and back end wiggles, he is licking a face.

I hold my breath, peering to the side to see bright red on what I presume might be legs. A man?

The wind whips and the boat rocks. To stay butted up against the berg, I have to keep the paddle dipped and constantly moving to push in the right direction.

I should be up there, helping Rigel. I can't expect a dog to revive a person, but would I be much more use?

Then a high bark from Rigel, a constant ticking wag of the tail. He even tips forward so his back forms a downward slope and then springs up, excited, as if he wants to play.

The figure on the ice sits up.

The figure on the ice is alive.

'Hey! Hey there!' I call out, and then with some difficulty the person starts to stagger towards me, stiff, like they are moving by clockwork.

I gasp, frozen in fright.

The thing that is staggering towards me doesn't look like a person at all, red feet and legs, then a black outline with no sign of arms. Plus the shape of its head is huge, and all wrong.

In a slice of panic I remember a few years back my brother scared me and Sarah half silly by reading parts of *Frankenstein's Monster or The Modern Prometheus* to us before Mother found out. Frank told us the monster was still out on the ice now, wandering, searching for a companion . . .

Oh, for goodness' sake. There's no such thing.

'Hello!' calls a voice more cracked than mine, and his steps become steadier.

'Hello!' I call out with a wave. 'Are you all right?'

'Officer Greeve!' I say, nudging the slumped man with my foot. The officer's eyes are only half open. I have a vague memory that you shouldn't let an injured person go to sleep. Panic grasps at my chest. I make my voice loud and firm.

'Third Officer Greeve, you are the ranking officer on this ship and we have found a *Titanic* survivor,' I say. 'The last survivor.'

The officer grunts, tries to sit up but his face crumples in pain.

Rigel wags along beside the strange figure on the iceberg and rests a hand on the dog's head. It's a boy. When he comes properly into view I can see it's a bizarre bundle of ill-fitting clothing that made him look so strange, including a headdress rather than a hat. Only a small part of his face is visible, but he's younger than my youngest older brother. Just a boy, all on his own out here. I blink. He doesn't seem ill or hurt.

Look what Rigel has done.

Without the dog this boy – now just ten feet from me – would die out here.

What had started as a mistake became a voyage, followed by a disastrous adventure, and now it is a mission.

A rescue mission.

41

'Oh, well done, Rigel! Good boy, good boy,' I say. The black dog's tail wags more quickly and he takes little skips. I suddenly feel a bit awkward in front of this stranger.

'Come aboard, I'm Clara Scott, good to meet you,' I say as the boy reaches the side of the boat. I hold out a hand – the other still gripping the oar keeping us steady in the sea – and he takes it, his encased in a chunky grey mitten. He sits quickly, pushing the strange headgear back from a face white as the icebergs that loom around us.

'Thank you. Thank you . . . miss. I'm Sid, Sidney Daniels, third-class steward on *Titanic*.'

The boat rocks and I sit too as Rigel leaps in and licks my hand.

The boy pats Rigel and his eyes meet mine. We manage a weak smile, then we both look at the officer.

'Pleased to meet you, sir,' he says doubtfully. As rescue missions go, I think we're a bit of a disappointment.

Third Officer Greeve tries to straighten up, face scrunching, grey with pain.

'He's broken his arm,' I say quietly and pull a face to show it is bad.

'I am Third Officer Greeve and I insist we return to the *Carpathia*,' mutters the officer.

The boy pats his lumpy clothing and brings out a silver hip flask. I raise my eyebrows.

'Oh, it's not mine, I found it in this coat pocket,' he says, and hands the flask to Officer Greeve, who takes a shaky swig and coughs.

I pull in the oar and lay it next to the other.

'Well this is Rigel, we are from the *Carpathia*,' I say – waving in the direction we came from, remembering he'll probably have no idea what I'm talking about. 'It's a steamship. It picked up the lifeboats from the *Titanic*, but Rigel here sensed you.'

The boy's mouth drops open. 'There's a ship, and the

people in the lifeboats are safe? All of them?'

I nod and shrug at the same time. 'All the ones we found are safe, I think,' I say.

'And your *Carpathia*, I mean, there were a lot of people in the water, a lot still on the *Titanic*, did you see, were you able to . . .'

I shake my head, biting my lip.

'Thank you, Clara. You – and Third Officer Greeve – saved my life,' he says, blinking his wide eyes.

'Oh, that was Rigel,' I say with a wave of my hand, feeling awkward.

'Well, you are the ones in the boat,' he argues and grins.

I look away from the boy, Sid, and out across the sea, white with ice. Large icebergs loom around us. We are three tiny figures and a dog in an ice field. The elation I felt at finding Sid is starting to fade.

'Are you any good at rowing?' I say.

'Not bad,' he says, 'but it's been a while.'

The wind has picked up, the sea ice knocks at the boat. We take an oar each and start pushing our way through. But Rigel leaps to the back of the boat, giving us a face full of fur as he passes.

'He'll have us all in,' says Third Officer Greeve, who sits up now, looking slightly revived and very cross.

'He's showing us the way,' I say, impatient.

We have only taken a couple of strokes when something nudges the boat.

I open my mouth but before I can say a word, the boat rises, pushed upwards, leaving my stomach behind. We slap back down in a plume of water and ice.

My eyes connect with Sid's, and Rigel releases a flurry of barks.

42

Rigel bounds to the front of the tender, barking and barking.

'Maybe it was ice,' I say. 'Maybe we were pushed up by some underwater . . . ice.'

'What are you waiting for, get moving,' says Officer Greeve.

Sid nods, his strange hat slipping over his eyes and then both at once, we row as hard as we can; side by side, elbow to elbow, leaning forward and pushing back, somehow completely in time.

I feel Sid fall still before he speaks.

'I . . . I just hit something with the oar,' he says, 'not one of those bergs, not ice, something else, underwater.'

This time I'm expecting it, and it definitely isn't ice.

The boat rises at the stern, higher and higher. I grasp on to the rails and Sid falls sideways into the bottom of the boat, beneath one of the benches, and screams.

Just as I think we will be tipped vertically and pitched in, whatever was underneath us falls away and the tender drops again, like a stone, splatting into the water so hard it jerks me up off the seat.

Sid dives forward, grasping both my legs, yanking me down to the bottom of the boat. The wave of water we've created splashes up around us, over us.

'There's something there,' I say, stupidly, 'something underneath us.'

Sid releases my legs and we huddle together into a crouch.

'I suppose it could be a whale?' says Sid. 'Or porpoises – dolphins?'

Third Officer Greeve: 'You need to keep rowing, the change in weather . . .'

I ignore him and nod my reply to Sid. 'We saw dolphins around the ship.'

'Were they big?' he says.

I nod. But nowhere near as big as something else. The thing I've been trying not to think about.

The creature. The monster. The sea serpent.

'Let's just stay completely still for a moment, maybe it will go away?' I say.

Me and Sid continue to hunch together and it should be weird that we are strangers to each other and this boy – barely a couple of years older than me by the looks of him – is so close I can feel his breath on my cheek. What's weirder is that it isn't strange at all.

Rigel barks and barks and I fancy it's the same bark I heard when I first met him, when he first tried to tell me what was out there. If the sea serpent is below us, why doesn't the dog sound afraid?

Another thud, this time against the side of the boat, shunting us.

Sid gasps and his breath becomes ragged, his lips tremble and he shakes.

'I'm sorry, you must think I'm awful lily-livered,' he whispers through chattering teeth, 'but I can't go in the water again, not again.'

I reach out a hand, unable to imagine what he has just been through. The *Titanic* foundered, sank, dark freezing water. And then all alone on that iceberg. He grips my fingers through the thick wool of his mittens. I see what I thought were mittens are actually long socks.

'You aren't in the least lily-livered. You survived. And you just stopped me being thrown in. In this get-up I'd sink like a stone,' I whisper, indicating the thick black oilskins.

'Yeah, you probably would,' he whispers back with a smile on his trembling lips, 'you look like a big black . . . slug.'

'Well you've got socks on your hands and what on earth is on your feet?' I say quietly into his ear. Through our held hands I feel him calming.

'More socks on top of shoes. It's survival fashion,' he says, and we both grin.

I release his hand.

'Do you think it's gone?' he says.

'If it wanted us in the water I think it's big enough to have already put us in there, don't you?'

Sid looks horrified for a moment and I realize it's probably not the most comforting thing to say. He shoots me an uncertain smile. 'You certainly have a way of looking on the bright side.'

Officer Greeve breaks in. 'I command you to keep rowing,' he says.

Sid draws a deep breath, the wind whistles around our ears, the boat bobs and Rigel barks again.

'And silence your dog!' hisses Officer Greeve.

'He's trying to tell us something,' I whisper. 'I think I know what it is down there.'

My mind draws a complete blank on how to explain it

to Sid, or even worse, Third Officer Greeve.

I am almost certain there is a sea serpent under our rowing boat.

And the one thing I do know about animals is that they do things for a reason and they all have a basic instinct in common.

They need to eat.

I decide there is no point telling this poor boy that after he's survived the *Titanic* I suspect we might be eaten by a sea serpent. By a creature that should only exist in myth.

Sid and me crouch together in the tender for a few more seconds waiting for another shove, or to finally be tipped in. The boat rocks as it is blown along, drifting hopefully in the right direction, small floaters of ice surrounding us so densely now as the wind gathers them, it's like a hovering, broken jigsaw puzzle.

A ram to the side of the boat; water rains over us.

It is no use keeping quiet with Rigel's constant barking, especially when he bounds on the prow of the boat looking as if he's about to jump.

'No, Rigel, no!' I stand, legs wide to keep balance, saying to Sid, 'Stay there.'

Could the monster leap from the water, pluck me out of the boat? I swallow hard. What's wrong with Rigel? Why isn't he afraid?

I peer over the side of the boat. Between the slabs of ice I see something that looks like rope, narrow frayed rope. A churn of water clears the ice for a moment.

Underneath, there is dark grey skin, smooth. An underwater body, unbelievably huge.

I gasp, unable to take my eyes off the sea serpent.

The rope is criss-crossed. A fishing net.

I follow the dark mass of the creature and it stretches beneath the water many times longer than the tender. Could a beast this big be tangled in a net?

'What are you doing?' says Sid from behind me and I hear him gasp.

The serpent now floats to the surface.

The grey-green net encases a huge smooth head that narrows, but not to a point. It looks a bit like pictures I've seen of snakes, but also like the head of an orca. Tiny eyes peer up at us through the lattice of the net as it floats on the surface. Its skin shines deepest blue-grey and there's that lighter grey line I caught sight of before, almost like hair or seaweed all along its back. Its whole body now breaks the surface and I see it's the girth of a large stallion but longer than ten horses, maybe more.

And its teeth.

Some small against the bulk of it, some as long as my whole hand. Two snaggled rows. Sharp.

Sid gasps and grabs my shoulder, rocking the boat. 'Clara, get down!'

I shrug free and Sid sits, gripping the sides of the tender, peering up at me white-faced.

'What. Is. That?' he whispers, lips trembling.

'I demand you row on!' says Officer Greeve, but I'm beginning not to even hear him any more. He can't help us, and he can't stop us.

'It's an . . . animal . . . a huge sea animal, I think it's caught in a net. Sid – will you help me get it free?'

The boy looks up at me in disbelief.

It all suddenly makes a crazy kind of sense to me. The serpent has been circling the *Carpathia* all along, and Rigel sensed it was in trouble. Maybe his barks even kept it close by.

Could it have been making contact with humans because that's where the net came from?

I grab the oar and slide it carefully into the water.

'Help me row closer to its head, Sid. Now!'

Sid shakes his head but does as I say and we pull alongside the end of the floating beast, to its huge head. The sight of it, the hugeness, the strangeness, sets my heart racing.

My hands tremble. I know how animals can act when in pain . . .

I mutter to myself, 'Just like an injured horse, it's only angry because it's hurting.'

Then I remember. Being at the farm, Gramma's old mare baring her teeth at me, her telling me if a horse is bad-tempered you check its feet. The hoof pick. The hoof pick that got me free of the trunk when I met Rigel. I know I still have it, it's been a comfort, reminding me of home. I slip my arms inside the heavy oilskins easily, as they are far too big and secured by a belt of rope around my waist. I dig around underneath, find the pocket in my jacket and bring out the hook.

'What on earth have you got there?' says Sid in a horrified voice.

I can't reply. If I get this wrong, I might kill us all. 'Just keep us steady,' I say to Sid and I ignore what he says next as I concentrate on sliding the oar beneath the edge of the rope. I lift the net, not wanting to spook the serpent, not wanting it to already be too late.

Then with the other hand – bracing myself on the side of the tender with my hips, both arms at work – I catch the hook of the hoof pick under the edge of the netting.

'Got it,' I say with a burst of energy and triumph. 'Sid, move to the other side to balance us so I can lean over a little more.'

Both Sid and Third Officer Greeve speak at once: 'This is insanity!'

'Clara! Please – please don't . . .'

'Sid, I need you to do this . . .' I say, and I want to yell, to make him do this because it has to work and I can't bear that yet another person doesn't trust me. But I calm down instead and make my voice as quiet as I can.

'Sid, I live on a farm and I know about injured animals, I am going to set this one free. It's been here our whole crossing, I think it's because it's in trouble. I rescued you, didn't I? Now I'm rescuing this creature.'

I look into his terrified eyes – and who can blame him for being so scared? But he meets my gaze and nods.

A groan from Greeve, and his head flops to the side. The officer is in a bad way.

'Now lean over the other side. Please.'

I don't give him a chance to argue, but lean over the side myself, hoping Sid will balance the boat with his weight. He does.

I reach down and slide the smooth loop of the hoof pick across the beast's skin. I clamber to the rear of the tender, hauling the net with me, then try to tug it off the sea serpent's neck. Some of it comes, but something is stuck. I'm not strong enough.

I look up at Rigel, still barking at the bow of the boat.

I remember the captain telling me he belonged to a fisherman. This dog swam in the wake of the steamer, swam all the way to Sid. But now I'm asking him to brave a monster, a myth come to life.

And he's just a dog.

But he's not scared.

'Rigel,' I say, and the dog turns and fixes me with those black intelligent eyes. If I say it as a question, maybe I'm letting him decide for himself.

'Rigel, can you fetch the net?'

Rigel springs into the water and swims away, his black head ploughing through the chunks of ice as he turns around at the end of the beast – I suppose its tail – and swims back towards me. With the serpent now between us, he paddles to the head. I pull again at the net and the serpent gives a weak twist of its long body. I don't know whether to be glad it is still alive, terrified it will have us all in or horrified that it's capable of eating Rigel in one bite.

'Fetch the net, Rigel,' I call and Rigel immediately grasps the net in his jaws. He pulls but the net doesn't come free.

Then Rigel does something I've never seen before. He dives down. I watch the surface where he went, the ice chunks closing over him. How long has it been? Can dogs dive like that?

'Rigel! Come up, come back! Rigel!'

Could the dog be caught in the net too? Will they both die and the boat will tip and that will be the end of me and Sid and Greeve as well?

All my idea, all my fault.

Then the serpent rolls, rocking the boat. And Rigel pings to the surface some way away, panting, the rope still in his jaws. He's pulled it free from underneath the giant's neck. This fisherman's dog knows how to wrestle a net.

With us both pulling, maybe it will all be released.

But the net is stuck in one place. The wind is so strong now, and blowing icy flicks of rain into my face. I push back the sou'wester and rub the water from my eyes, then remember Sid.

'You are doing great – sorry – you might need to lean out a bit more!'

I don't look round or wait for an answer.

Leaning further over the edge of the boat, I slot my leg under one of the benches.

This is crazy, I know. Sid is calling something out to that effect and I feel sorry for that. But I can't stop now.

I reach down so I can touch the surface of the sea serpent's skin. I want to recoil back at the strangeness of it. Not as smooth as it looks – a slightly rough surface one way – but then when I stroke towards its tail my hand slips over the surface like silk.

I didn't expect it to be warm. It's an animal, alive.

I tug on the hook holding the rope and see that below and behind the serpent's eyes are a row of slices in the skin. I hate preparing fish, but I've had to do it a few times when my brothers took me camping by the river for the night. The flaps are its gills used for breathing water, and there is something stuck in one of them.

The sea serpent might be a monster and a myth but it's also just an animal that can't breathe properly.

I swallow and pull my glove off with my teeth, so I can keep one hand on the hook with the net attached. The freezing air and water sting like needles on my hand but only for a moment before my skin is numb. I won't have long before I can't use my fingers at all. I slide my hand down the rope to where it leads inside one of the gill openings. Warm water gushes out and I find something with my fingers. Something round and hard. I tug and the beast rolls, almost pulling me in. The boat rocks, Rigel barks, Sid yells.

'Sorry,' I whisper and this time I slide my fingers around the trapped object, pressing against the beast's warm flesh; my whole hand disappears into the serpent and I have to fight an almost unbearable urge to snatch it back, imagining this huge body closing around my hand and swallowing it. Or being trapped, held tight, as the serpent swims away, dragging me with it.

I grip the stone with my numb fingers, grit my teeth, and twist it as carefully as I can.

A burst of blood into the water.

Sea serpent's blood is red, same colour as mine.

The stone pings free, and the net with it.

It is a stone as big as the palm of my hand with a hole through the middle, through which the rope of the net is threaded. A weight. A weight made to help a net sink has brought this creature to the surface.

I drop the stone and the net pulls loose, hauled down into the ocean, gone.

The sea serpent is free.

I sit now on the bench of the tender, watching the beast's huge body sink into the choppy water.

'Rigel – come now,' I call and the dog, who has been circling near the head of the animal, swims to the stern of the tender. I wince as Rigel passes those teeth. Sid and I both move forward to counterbalance as Rigel leaps up and gives an almighty shake-off.

Sid sits next to me. 'You did it,' he says, a smile in his voice.

I don't answer, as I scan the water for a sign, the boat swaying without the steadying of the oars. Is the animal dead and sunk?

'It was no good, I was too late.'

The unconscious Greeve is slumped in the bottom of the boat. He looks young, helpless. Is it too late for him too?

I'm surprised to feel tears, and brush them away with the heel of my hand.

'It's probably swum away, and I don't mind telling you that I'm not sorry about that,' says Sid. 'Here,' he says. 'Put this back on or you'll get frostbite.'

I hold out my hand. The tips of my fingers are numb and an alarming waxy white colour. He slides on my glove.

'Now I suppose we row?' he says.

I look around and everything looks the same: icebergs in the distance, medium-sized bergs dotted around, some bigger than the boat, then that scattered layer across the surface of smaller pieces of ice.

If the wind has changed direction then who knows where we are rowing? But there's no point in saying that to Sid.

'It's this way, I think – the ice field is moving but the *Carpathia* is anchored, we're blowing right towards it.'

Sid bites his lip, and nods. He knows I don't have a clue.

We start to haul the oars together anyhow.

After around twenty strokes, once again getting into a good rhythm with Sid, we spot something at the same time.

The *Carpathia*.

45

Sid and I call out at the same time, backsides bouncing on the bench. The head of unconscious Greeve bobbles from side to side and his eyes open.

'We are here! Here!' I yell. 'Look Officer Greeve, you need to wake up, it's *Carpathia*.'

We both wave. They surely have lookouts with eyeglasses trained this way.

Rigel barks, standing once again at the prow.

Relief washes over me so suddenly my knees are weak. We did it.

The wind batters into my back and waves rock us,

knocking together the ice all around.

A large iceberg with two peaks drifts ahead.

The wind has taken us now, we barely need to row, but this beast of an ice island is barely moving. And it's in our path.

'We need to swerve around it,' I say. 'Keep rowing!'

Sid stares up at the looming berg, now blocking our view of *Carpathia*, and falls still.

'That's it. That's it! The one. *Titanic*.'

The boy's mouth falls open, the oar loose in his hand, but we need to row on that side if the wind isn't going to shoot us right into the giant berg. I climb across Sid, who continues to stare, dumbstruck, and snatch up his oar.

Rigel barks, over and over, the rhythmical bark I've come to know so well, trying to tell me something, but I don't see how he can help us now.

'Here, son,' says Third Officer Greeve who has revived enough to shove the hip flask beneath Sid's nose.

The boy ignores it, continuing to stare at the iceberg, muttering. 'It hit us. We played with the ice.'

'He thinks it's the iceberg that sank the *Titanic*, but I don't see—'

'Oh, shut up, will you!' I yell at the officer.

I start rowing again, but the wind is now so strong I can't direct the boat alone, can't steer at all.

Then a bump against the hull. The pieces of ice on

the surface slide to the sides to reveal that slick massive body. The sea serpent is back.

Its blunt head bursts from the surface and I swear it stares straight at me with those shining slit-pupil eyes. Have I set it free just so it can follow its most basic need, to eat us? I hold the oar out of the water and push down on the handle of Sid's too, so both oars spread out of the water like wings. An almighty nudge almost knocks us sideways as I stare in horror at the iceberg.

Pushed to the side and round, lifted clean from the sea, the tender spins on the back of the sea serpent and all three of us scream. We shoot around the side of the berg, the looming ice towering above, but almost in touching distance.

Then we plunge down, the water floating us off the sea serpent's back, facing the wrong way. Wind and waves hit the side of the boat and I drop my oar. The creature sinks again into the icy sea.

Everything seems to slow, and I realize a lot of things at once.

The serpent nudges us again, nose to the side of the boat, spinning us so we face away from the wind.

We can't row but a surging wave, or the serpent, shoots us forward. We skim the edge of the iceberg that sank the *Titanic*.

The sea serpent is alongside, slick skin shining.

A shot rings out.

I spin around.

Third Officer Greeve crouches in the back of the boat, heavily panting, a pistol in his good hand. Then another shot, hitting a chunk of ice and breaking it, so ice sprays in our faces.

Sid's voice. 'He's got a gun?'

I scream, 'No! Stop!'

I drop the oar, dive over the bench and haul Greeve's hand into the air. We struggle just like we once did with the oar, but I'm stronger now, even without momentum on my side. I crack the back of his hand against the side of the ship. The gun arcs through the air and plops into the water.

It's only then I realize that Rigel is in the sea.

Scarlet blood splatters the sea ice that surrounds the huge black dog.

46

Sid holds me back from leaping into the sea after Rigel. For a long moment I can't think – it must be a fatal shot, the dog is motionless.

My dog. My Rigel, now so small in the grey ocean, closed in by the blood-splashed ice...

But Rigel circles, barks once and paddles slowly towards the boat.

He attempts to leap up but something is wrong; his front paws meet the edge of the boat but when his back legs don't follow in his usual bound, he slips back into the sea. He circles again.

'Help him!'

Sid and I somehow manage to heave the drenched black dog into our boat. Blood splatters everywhere when he shakes.

I quickly find the wound; it's to his back leg, a long channel across the surface.

'It's a flesh wound,' yells Sid over the battering wind. 'Clara – it's a flesh wound, he's all right.'

I'm sobbing, and swallow down my tears. I hold the dog's face, kiss his salty nose and hug him tight, then Sid rips a fancy-looking silk scarf from around his neck. The fingers on my right hand are completely numb from being under the freezing water for so long freeing the sea serpent, but between us, Sid and I wrap and tie the scarf tightly around Rigel's leg.

The bleeding stops.

We sit with the huge dog between us, both our arms around his neck. I glare at the now-collapsed Third Officer Greeve.

He exhausted himself trying to kill what he didn't understand.

A boat has been launched from the *Carpathia*. They are coming to get us, we just need to sit tight.

I wish there was no such thing as a gun.

The weather doesn't get any better, but at least it doesn't

get any worse. We are soon lifted into the other boat by two strong sailors. Greeve remains in the blood-splashed tender, towed behind. It isn't long before one of the sailors yells to tell us the *Carpathia* is in front of us. I can hardly believe it. After a bit of discussion, Rigel and I are hauled up the side of the ship squashed together in the same burlap sack, followed by Sid who is too weak to climb the ladder.

Harold drags me to my feet, enclosing me in a hug, then holding me at arm's length.

'Is that blood? Are you injured—'

'No no – I'm fine, it's Rigel, we need to get him fixed up. But honestly, I'm all right.'

Harry blows out, giving me a little shake. 'You are in one piece, Clarty. Blooming heck, I thought we'd lost you. You brave crazy girl.'

He releases me and then stays close. With my hand buried in Rigel's neck fur, and Sid being fussed over, wrapped in blankets, I wait for the two sailors to climb up.

'I think it's best we get you both inside—' But I shake my head.

I'm waiting for Third Officer Greeve.

The injured officer is hauled aboard in a burlap sack like we were. His father, Chief Steward First Class Mr Greeve-Birtwistle, barges through the crowd and grasps his son's arms.

I'll give father and son this moment before I spoil the reunion.

I wait to see Mr Greeve-Birtwistle's relief that his son is alive, his concern for him being injured, but he smirks, eyes sparkling.

'You are a hero, son, let me deal with this,' he mutters, then calls out, 'Third Officer Greeve found the last *Titanic* survivor!'

Some of the gathering crowd whisper and there are a few claps.

Hero? Sid's eyebrows rise at the same time as mine.

'It was Rigel who found Sid, and you shot him!' I say.

This time a gasp from the crowd.

'Look,' I say, pointing at Rigel's wound.

'Absolute nonsense,' yells Mr Greeve-Birtwistle, 'this young officer is a hero. And I'd like to know how he came by his injury. I'll wager it was to do with this stowaway.'

I can't believe what I'm hearing. 'Greeve! Tell everyone what happened, right now.'

The officer groans and leans hard upon his father, a triumphant glint finding me from under his eyelids. The third officer knows exactly what he is doing.

Greeve-Birtwistle continues, 'This young ne'r-do-well has caused nothing but trouble on this boat. Nothing but trouble since she stowed away, and I caught her thieving from the hold. It is blatantly obvious she is now trying to take the glory for this miraculous rescue herself.'

I glance at Sid. Surely he's going to tell them the truth, but instead he's raking through his pockets.

The crowd around us murmur and shift. I see the friendly faces of some who saw Rigel helping the *Titanic* survivors; others like Yolanda and John's mother shake their heads, disapproving.

Then Captain Rostron is next to me. 'Welcome aboard, young man,' he says.

'. . . Sid Daniels, sir, third-class steward, *Titanic*,' says Sid, leaning against me and wincing as he shakes the captain's hand. I think his feet are hurt.

'Captain,' says Mr Greeve-Birtwistle. 'I'm afraid Miss Scott is telling a string of lies, slanderous accusations against Third Officer Greeve, the very man who saved this boy's life. You obviously will not stand for it.'

'I will hear what the girl has to say,' says the captain.

I explain calmly what happened. When Greeve-Birtwistle interrupts, the captain silences him with a raise of the hand.

'My officers are not permitted to carry arms aboard. Do you have any evidence for your version of events, Miss Scott?' says Captain Rostron, frowning.

'The bullet wound – on Rigel's leg!' I yell triumphantly.

'Caused by a shard of ice, no doubt,' counters Mr Greeve-Birtwistle. 'Ice sank the *Titanic*, so I'm sure it can scratch a dog.'

The man grins at his own joke, but considering plenty of the surrounding people are *Titanic* survivors, I hear tuts and see frowns. He might be losing the support of the crowd, but there's going to be no proof of what Greeve did.

'I can't show you the gun because I knocked it into the ocean, before he hurt someone else,' I say.

'Absolute nonsense,' says Greeve-Birtwistle.

And then I realize. I am not going to win here. The unfairness of it sweeps over me and I lean against Sid. At least he is safe, even if he can't speak up for me, and Rigel will be all right.

But it seems Sid does have something to say for himself.

'Captain Rostron?' he says. 'I think you should have this.' He holds up a piece of metal between his thumb and forefinger. A bullet casing.

2.10 P.M.
FROM: CARPATHIA
TO: OLYMPIC

ON ARRIVAL AT DAYBREAK WE SAW ICE 25
MILES LONG, SOLID QUANTITY WRECKAGE
AND NUMBER OF BOATS FULL OF LIVES.

WE RAISED ABOUT SIX HUNDRED AND
SEVENTY SOULS. TITANIC HAD SUNK SHE
WENT DOWN IN TWO HOURS.

FROM: OLYMPIC
TO: CARPATHIA

KINDLY INFORM ME IF THERE IS THE
SLIGHTEST HOPE IN SEARCHING TITANIC
POSITION

FROM: CARPATHIA
TO: OLYMPIC

DON'T ATTEMPT TO GO NORTH UNTIL
49.30 W MANY BERGS LARGE AND SMALL
AMONGST PACK. FEAR ABSOLUTELY NO
HOPE SEARCHING TITANIC'S POSITION.

UNITED STATES SENATE INQUIRY

Day 10 - 28th April 1912
Testimony of Sidney Daniels

SOLICITOR GENERAL: So if we could carry on where you left off, Mr Daniels?

SENATOR BOURNE: Mr Daniels? Are you all right? Do you need a little time?

- No, sir. Just - trying to remember. I'd managed to climb on top of the iceberg. I pulled the suitcase after me and changed into the clothes from the suitcase.

SENATOR BOURNE: Take your time, son, there's water on the desk if you need it.

- Thank you, sir. I dressed in as many dry clothes as I could, nearly every single item in the suitcase, and then curled up on the life jackets that I'd taken from the raft. That was to keep out the cold of the ice.

SOLICITOR GENERAL: And that's how you survived longer than any other passenger - some say no one survived more than forty minutes in the water - although others report two hours, we believe it may be much less than that.

- I believe it, sir, the cold was - something else. But I was in a kind of dip on the iceberg and although I wasn't warm, I slept. Then Clara - Miss Scott - arrived with Rigel the dog and we rowed towards the Carpathia.

SOLICITOR GENERAL: And Third Officer Greeve?

- Oh. Yes. He was there too, although too injured to help.

SOLICITOR GENERAL: What were the conditions at this point?

- We were in the middle of the ice field, surrounded by hunks of ice of all sizes and huge icebergs in every direction. The wind had picked up too.

SOLICITOR GENERAL: So how did you locate the Carpathia and make it safely out of the ice?

- I actually don't know, sir. I was very cold and shocked and not wholly myself. Clara maybe followed a flare? But I couldn't say for sure.

SOLICITOR GENERAL: But it was broad daylight when you were picked up by the Carpathia, she couldn't have followed a flare.

- I'm sure I don't know, sir.

SENATOR BOURNE: Thank you, Mr Daniels. Do you have anything more to add?

- No, sir. It was a blur, I was very cold.

SENATOR BOURNE: So let me get this clear. Shortly after you were marooned in the ice field and changed into the clothes in the suitcase you happened to find, and that happened to be dry, Miss Scott - who is a twelve-year-old girl with no experience of rowing, or boating in general and certainly not navigation, who is in fact a farm girl, and cannot swim - arrived in a tender, passed through the ice floes alone - as the only adult in this escapade was injured - and rescued you. Oh - and she had this dog with her?

- Er, yes, sir. Did you say Clara can't swim? She never told me that.

SENATOR BOURNE: Now. You've shared such impressive detail of your duties on board, the days running up to the Titanic's sinking and your experience of the sinking itself. But there's only very scant detail of how you not only navigated through the huge icebergs reported, but also made it to meet the rescue lifeboat.

- We must have been very lucky with the . . . currents.

SENATOR BOURNE: Anything at all you would like to add?

- Nothing, sir. Nothing at all.

16TH APRIL
FROM: NEW YORK
TO: CARPATHIA

WILL BE WORRIED TO DEATH TILL I
HEAR FROM YOU. WHAT AWFUL AGONY.
JULIE

17TH APRIL
FROM: NEW YORK
TO: CARPATHIA

WORRIED TO DEATH. PLEASE WIRE IF
SAFE AND CONDITION AT ONCE.
J E BRULATOUR

FROM: CARPATHIA
TO: NEW YORK

LEILA SAFE AND WELL CARED FOR.
EDGAR MISSING.

18TH APRIL
FROM: CARPATHIA

TO: JULES E BRULATOUR

SAFE PICKED UP BY CARPATHIA. DON'T
WORRY. DOROTHY.

FROM: CARPATHIA
TO: NEW YORK

EVERY BOAT WATCHED, FATHER.
MOTHER NOT ON CARPATHIA.
HOPE STILL.
BADENOCH

FROM: CARPATHIA
TO: NEW YORK

BOTH SAVED. MOTHER.

FROM: CARPATHIA
TO: NEW YORK

DON'T BE ALARMED SYDNEY MAY BE ON
ANOTHER BOAT.
JACOBSON

FROM: CARPATHIA

TO: PHILADELPHIA

FATHER NOT SEEN. NO HOPE. ARRIVE
CARPATHIA WEDNESDAY NEW YORK.
RICHARD

28th

April

1912

'Not bad,' I say. 'At least better than last time . . . which was shocking.'

I lead Bess to the water trough and Sid swings down from the saddle on to the horse block, wincing at his sore foot. He glares at me from beneath my brother's wide-brim hat, which he says makes him feel like a real cowboy. Both our faces are speckled with the red dust of the paddock.

'When you're teaching someone you're supposed to give encouragement,' he says.

'You're learning, aren't you?' I retort and we grin at each other.

Sid has been staying with us while he recovers enough, first to give his testimony, and now until he's fit to work back on board another ocean liner. Everyone has been making a meal of him being here, the last crew member to leave *Titanic*, the last survivor to be found . . . for days my brothers chased reporters off the ranch.

To me he's not a miracle, he's just my friend.

'Is your foot sore?' I say, as I take his arm on one side.

'Ah – only a scratch,' he says. 'What about your finger?'

'What finger?' I say, holding up the bandaged stump.

We laugh. I lost half a finger to frostbite and Sid lost part of three toes. At first we would compare notes from our beds that Ma confined us to, me insisting that I'd much rather lose toes than a finger and what was all the fuss about. Sid retorting that at least I could walk. But since we've been allowed up and about we prefer to pretend we can't feel it at all, and secretly I feel more sorry for Sid.

My sister waves from the house. She has a package. I see her give it to the fluffy black mound that sleeps in the shade of the veranda.

Rigel healed first, his wound already just a narrow scar. He isn't really built for the heat of the ranch but he's getting used to it. I refused to let my brothers shear him like a sheep but Ma and my sisters helped trim and comb out his undercoat so he could be more comfortable. He now looks more like a bear than ever with his short fuzzy hair. The hotel owner in Sicily who was left him in the will was contacted by the now-famous captain of the *Titanic* rescue ship himself – Captain Rostron – and it didn't take much persuasion for him to sign the hero dog Rigel over to the Scott family.

My dog trots towards me, package in his soft mouth, and I kneel to fuss him. He licks my nose as I turn it over. From Bernie Palmer? On the journey back to New York we became rather peculiar, but also rather good . . . friends.

I draw out a sheaf of photographs. Of the survivors, of the icebergs, of Sid and I in our strange outfits after we were brought on board.

Dear Clara (and hopefully Sid if you're still at the ranch),

These photos are the ones I've sold to the newspaper, and they will be published any day now. But the photo in the envelope I only have three copies of.

One for me. I won't ever sell this one and you know why.

One for you and Sid.

One for Captain Rostron.

Keep writing, you know I'll be coming to visit.

I won't say keep out of trouble because what would be the point!

Bernie

I open the sealed envelope.

It was taken as we rowed up to the *Carpathia*, the two sailors in the front of the boat, me, Rigel and Sid behind them, Third Officer Greeve towed behind in the other boat. It still makes me angry to look at him. Blood splatters don't show up in black and white, but I'll always see the red.

Rigel rolls in the dust and I sit cross-legged next to him and rub his belly. 'Silly big boy, aren't you.' He does that a lot these days, playful now he's not always on watch.

Rigel – brightest star in the sky, navigated us home safe, and found his own home too.

When this shot was taken everyone on deck was looking at us, the stowaway girl, the ownerless dog and the injured officer. And at Sid Daniels, last crew member to escape *Titanic*, almost lost in the ice field.

But Bernie's photo has also captured the unbelievable. Against a background canvas of icebergs and the jagged white edge of the ice field is a dark head, rising from the sea. The faintest glint of a snaggled tooth.

Another, even more miraculous survivor.

AUTHOR'S NOTE

This entire story is fictional, but is based on the
real experiences of the following people.

TRUE HEROES

Sidney Daniels – Third-Class Steward, RMS *Titanic*
In this story Sid Daniels is a fictional character based on a
real-life *Titanic* survivor. The real Sidney Edward Daniels
served as a third-class steward on *Titanic* and was the last
member of the crew to leave the ship and survive. He was
a teenager, but eighteen years old, so I've made him
younger, inspired by the youngest crew members on the
Titanic – Frederick William Hopkins (Plates Steward)
and William Albert Watson (Bellboy) were only fourteen, and tragically both died when the *Titanic* sank.

Out of 891 crew members on RMS *Titanic*, only 212
survived, less than a quarter. This was a higher death rate
than for the third-class passengers.

Sid Daniels helped launch a lifeboat that saved
twenty-four people. He managed to swim to an
upturned lifeboat – the one he had helped cut free as the
ship went down. This is the point where Sid's fictional
story begins, as he's swept away from that lifeboat and
into further adventure!

Rigel the Newfoundland Dog

It was only when I read the article below that I decided I definitely wanted to write a *Titanic* story. Unfortunately, it's unlikely Rigel the Newfoundland even existed. There were definitely dogs on the *Titanic*, but Rigel is not listed among them. What is more likely is that on the return to New York, many writers were hoping for an unusual *Titanic* story just like I was; the difference is, newspaper reporters are supposed to tell the truth!

There are records of Vikings bringing 'bear dogs' to North America over 1,500 years ago. These were then bred to help humans and named Newfoundlands in 1770 after a region in Canada where they were popular. With their webbed feet for swimming, thick warm coat and gentle protective personality, they were perfect working dogs. They used their strength to help Canadian fisherman pull heavy nets to shore, and even hauled carts of fish to market!

My – or I should say Clara's – Rigel is fictional, but the stories of heroic Newfoundlands are real. Just two Newfoundland heroes are Gander, who received the animal's Victoria Cross medal for his deeds in World War II, and Bilbo who worked as a lifeguard on the beaches of Cornwall, England until 2015. There are many more. Dogs truly are a human's best friend.

The New York Herald, **Sunday April 21st 1912**
*SURVIVOR'S CRIES WEAK, DOG'S BARK
CAUSES RESCUE OF BOATLOAD*

*Rigel, Whose Master Sank with the Titanic, Guides the
Carpathia's Captain to Suffering Passengers Hidden Under
Rescue Ship's Bow.*

Not the least among the heroes of the Titanic disaster
was Rigel, a big black Newfoundland dog, belonging to the
first officer, who went down with his ship. But for Rigel the
fourth boat picked up might have been run down by the
Carpathia. For three hours he swam in the icy water where
the Titanic went down, evidently looking for his master,
and was instrumental in guiding the boatload of survivors
to the gangway of the Carpathia.

Jonas Briggs, a sailor aboard the Carpathia, now has
Rigel and told the story of the dog's heroism. The
Carpathia was moving slowly about, looking for boats,
rafts, or anything which might be afloat. Exhausted with
their efforts, weak from lack of food and exposure to the
cutting wind, and terror stricken, the men and women in
the fourth boat had drifted under the Carpathia's starboard
bow. They were dangerously close to the steamship, but too
weak to shout a warning loud enough to reach the bridge.

The boat might not have been seen were it not for the
sharp barking of Rigel, who was swimming ahead of the

craft, and valiantly announcing his position. The barks attracted the attention of Captain Rostron and he went to the starboard end of the bridge to see where they came from and saw the boat. He immediately ordered the engines stopped and the boat came alongside the starboard gangway.

Care was taken to take Rigel aboard, but he appeared little affected by his long trip through the ice cold water. He stood by the rail and barked until Captain Rostron called Briggs and had him take the dog below.

Captain Arthur Rostron

When I read about brave and skilful Captain Rostron guiding his smaller ship through the treacherous ice fields to the rescue . . . I knew I had a special setting for most of my *Titanic* story – on the rescue ship *Carpathia*. Most people have heard of the tragedy of the *Titanic* disaster, but many have never heard of the smaller ship *Carpathia* that rescued the survivors. When I discovered the captain of this ship actually believed in sea monsters, this author couldn't believe her luck! The sea serpent of this story is based on the sightings that Captain Rostron described below. When he wrote this account he was a sensible not-at-all superstitious thirty-eight-year-old man, known for being calm and reliable, who had been serving on ships for twenty years.

In his memoirs *Home from the Sea* (pp. 45–47)

Commander Rostron tells how he was acting as Chief Officer on board the *Campania* on 26th April 1907, when something remarkable happened.

We were coming one Friday evening into Queenstown, when off Galley Head, I noticed something sticking out of the water. 'Keep clear of the snag right ahead,' I called out to the junior officer who was with me on the bridge. We swung away a point but gradually drew nearer so that we were able to make out what the unusual thing was. It was a sea monster! It was no more than fifty feet from the ship's side when we passed it, and so both I and the junior officer had a good sight of it.

So strange an animal was it that I remember crying out: 'It's alive!' One has heard such yarns about these monsters and cocked a speculative eye at the teller, that I wished as never before that I had a camera in my hands.

After delivering the *Titanic* survivors safely in New York, Captain Rostron was awarded a US Congressional Gold Medal by the President for his courage. The captain's kindness and care in looking after them was especially noted. He was also knighted by King George V in England.

Captain Rostron did not report any sightings of sea serpents during his heroic *Titanic* rescue mission, but that doesn't mean there wasn't one out there . . .

Bernice Palmer and Mrs Palmer

Bernice (Bernie) Palmer was given a Kodak 'brownie' camera shortly before she and her mother left Canada, bound for a Mediterranean cruise on the Carpathia. They were first-class cabin passengers, aboard the ship when it rescued the survivors of the *Titanic* disaster. Bernie took many photographs that would be published by newspapers back in New York, including the only one that showed the iceberg the *Titanic* may have hit.

Harold Cottam, Marconi Telegraph Operator

Harold was the youngest ever graduate from the British College of Telegraphy in London, finishing when he was still seventeen, and by the age of twenty-one he was working on RMS *Carpathia*. He didn't have a cousin called Clara, but everything else about his experience of the *Titanic* rescue I've tried to keep as close to the truth as possible. If he hadn't stayed up late waiting for a message from a different ship, he would never have received the distress call from *Titanic*. When *Carpathia* arrived in New York with the *Titanic* survivors, Harold was given a well-deserved hero's welcome.

Frederick Barratt

Frederick Barratt was a twenty-nine-year-old lead stoker on *Titanic*, managing the constant flow of coal to the furnaces that drove the huge engines. Barratt was put in charge of lifeboat 13, one of the fullest lifeboats taking sixty-five to seventy passengers, and the second to last to leave *Titanic*.

All other characters including Mr Greeve-Birtwistle, Third Officer Greeve, Mr Chan the barber, and of course Clara Scott and family, are purely products of my imagination.

THE CALL

The Electrical Telegraph and Morse Code

Until the 1840s, sending messages wasn't easy. The only options were: face-to-face conversations; sending coded messages, smoke signals or semaphore systems; or reading printed or handwritten words sent via letters on foot or horseback. These methods were unhurried and unreliable. Then Samuel F. B. Morse and other inventors developed the electrical telegraph in the 1830s and 1840s, and it would certainly speed things up. The telegraph worked by transmitting electrical signals over a wire laid between stations. Only trouble was, an electrical current by itself cannot make a message – it's invisible and silent, after all. But electricity can be converted into light or sound!

So Samuel Morse created a telegraph machine. It worked by pushing down a key – a kind of push switch – which completed an electrical circuit, sending an electrical signal across a wire to a receiver which converted it to sound. And all that at such a fast speed it was almost instant. It felt like a miracle! When he pushed the key down, there was a sound at the other end of the wire. When he released the key, there was a pause. But now he needed a language that could be communicated just by sounds and pauses. He invented Morse code, where letters are represented by combinations of pressing the key down for longer to make a dash or shorter to make a dot, with pauses in between. With Morse code you could also send messages by flashlight.

To begin with, Morse's telegraph machine would only work if there was a wire for the electricity to travel through. But in the late nineteenth century, Guglielmo Marconi invented radio-telegraph equipment, which could send Morse code over radio waves, rather than wires. Finally, ships could use it too, and young men like Harold Cottam of the *Carpathia* could be trained by Marconi's company to operate it. Without this brand-new technology, every single person in the *Titanic* lifeboats would have died.

MORSE CODE
(ALPHABETICAL)

A	• —		N	— •
B	— • • •		O	— — —
C	— • — •		P	• — — •
D	— • •		Q	— — • —
E	•		R	• — •
F	• • — •		S	• • •
G	— — •		T	—
H	• • • •		U	• • —
I	• •		V	• • • —
J	• — — —		W	• — —
K	— • —		X	— • • —
L	• — • •		Y	— • — —
M	— —		Z	— — • •
1	• — — — —		6	— • • • •
2	• • — — —		7	— — • • •
3	• • • — —		8	— — — • •
4	• • • • —		9	— — — — •
5	• • • • •		0	— — — — —

Radio Codes

To speed up the Morse code messages sent, the operators would use abbreviations. They are a bit like text speak! I have expanded some of the words so the messages make sense. The telegraph messages you read in the book are as accurate as I could make them, using the exact words but sometimes shortening to make them clearer. Here are some of the codes Harry Cottam and the other wireless operators used:

CQ	Calling all ships
CQD	Distress – Calling all ships
DDD	'Shut up' – this was often used because all the messages would come in at once and the operator couldn't hear what was being said!
G	Go ahead/start sending
K	Please reply
NR	No response
OM	'Old man' – a friendly way to greet operators, a bit like we'd use 'mate'
RD	Received
SOS	Distress (from 1908)
STD BI	Stand by/Please wait
TIS	End of message

A Tale of Two ships

Titanic

Carpathia

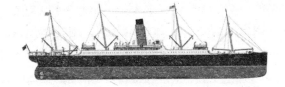

	Titanic	*Carpathia*
Length	882 feet/269 metres	540 feet/165 metres
Width	92 feet/28 metres	64 feet/20 metres
Tonnage	46,000	13,603
Max speed	23–24 knots	17 knots
Year built	1911	1901
Crew*	891	320
Passengers*	1,300 approx	740

*On this voyage

Titanic Lifeboats

Titanic carried sixteen wooden lifeboats on board and four collapsible lifeboats. These twenty boats could have accommodated 1,178 people, over half of those on board the night the ship sank. *Titanic*'s owners – White Star Line – decided not to take the sixty-four lifeboats that were needed to take all passengers the ship could carry, because they were not required to by the British Board of Trade. It was thought at the time that lifeboats could ferry passengers from the stricken ship to the rescuing ship, and then come back for more.

On the night of the tragedy only eighteen boats were launched the last two collapsibles floated off the deck. The lifeboats actually launched with even fewer people than they could take. Lifeboat 2 contained only twelve people. At the early stages of the lifeboat launch the passengers fully expected to be asked to return to the *Titanic*.

ACKNOWLEDGEMENTS

It took an entire crew of heroes to get this ship afloat!

With heartfelt thanks to:

My anchor and agent, Clare Wallace. I can't overstate the impact you've had, building me as a career author. Your vision, professionalism, savvy and sensitivity make it all happen. Thanks also to the superb team at Darley Anderson.

My life raft and editor, Rachel Leyshon. Yet again, my wild combination of history, adventure, mayhem and myth come together with your sterling guidance, trust, and profound understanding of what I'm trying to achieve. I can't even fathom how much I've learnt from you.

My publishing crew at Chicken House, Barry, Elinor, Jazz, Laura, Esther, Olivia, Kesia and all at Chicken House for your continued support, resourcefulness and imagination.

The cover watch, Rachel Hickman, Steve, Esther (again!) and magnificent artist Gordy Wright. Absolutely smashing the challenging design elements and aesthetic for this one. Thank you for all the work, discussion and dedication to getting it exactly right.

Call of the Titanic has been the trickiest book I've written so far – many months were sucked into a vortex of fascinating but truly harrowing research. Invaluable sources were:

'Titanic Belfast: The Titanic Experience and SS *Nomad*.' Expert staff, so good I visited twice.

'Titanic: The Exhibition', London. Immersive with a mesmerizing collection of artefacts.

'Marconi Archives: Special Collections', Bodleian Library, Oxford. Paging through the original wireless messages that feature in this book was a humbling experience.

Titanic Calling: Wireless Communications During The Great Disaster by Michael Hughes, senior archivist and published by Bodleian Library, University of Oxford, 2012, a constant source of reference. Andy Skinner, *Titanic* historian at SeaCity Museum, who read the final draft for historical acuracy. All mistakes my own.

Finally more thanks, to:

Gerry, Margaret and beautiful Newfoundland Mishka.

All my friends, the uni group, my ex-colleagues, neighbours and the Seaford girls who I went with on that first fateful trip to Belfast. And now your dazzling batch of growing kids . . . I am loving this new generation of cheerleader-readers.

My supporters online, particularly #edutwitter and the indie booksellers, bloggers and bookaholics. The brilliant #writementor and my inspiring mentees past and present, particularly stalwarts Claudia and Ann-Marie.

The teachers, librarians, event organizers and young people who have invited me to their classrooms and event spaces either in person or digitally. I have loved your company, and feel honoured to share stories with you.

To my writing friends online, and my writing retreat pals – Em, Jenni and Anna, all cherished writing colleagues.

Sarah Harris. Fellow rollercoaster rider, so glad to have you by my side.

Jo Hogan. My beta-reader and believer, wouldn't be doing this without you.

My best girl, Sally, and the Gassons for being my 'framily'.

The Moakes family, and in-laws, for always being there, Pam for the puzzles! The extended northern clan who all read and celebrate. My brother Rob for stories yet to come, and Jo, Arlo and Jem who scoop me up at zero notice.

My Galvin family, Mum, Dad, Kathryn, for the rescues and reads, the fun . . . and the fallback funding!

Gorgeous queens of fur, Flinny and Saffy.

Astonishing sons Edward and Oscar who I adore, and who need to remember their hats.

My true love, Bill, for all of it . . . and some.